Video Vengeance

By the same author

A Charmed Death
Cruel Victim
Some Predators are Male
Death of a Man-Tamer
The Frightened Wife
The Cords of Vanity

Video Vengeance

Miles Tripp

St. Martin's Press
New York

Library of Congress Cataloging-in-Publication Data

Tripp, Miles.
    Video vengeance / Miles Tripp.
        p.   cm.
    "A Thomas Dunne book."
    ISBN 0-312-05531-5
    I. Title.
  PR6070.R48V5   1991
  823'.914—dc20   90-49307
                                                                        CIP

First published in Great Britain by Macmillan London Limited

First U.S. Edition: January 1991
10 9 8 7 6 5 4 3 2 1

Video Vengeance

1

Samson's day began with limbering-up exercises in his bedroom followed by a brisk walk round St James's Park. This routine was part of a weight-reducing programme following a doctor's advice that he should shed at least thirty pounds. He was a naturally indolent man but to his surprise he found the routine enjoyable. It was pleasant to see waterfowl on the lake, banks of regimented flowers, tame pigeons and sparrows, swards of grass and the view of Buckingham Palace from the bridge. He also liked observing nine-to-five wage-mice as they scuttled to their daily treadwheel. It was a very different scene from the one he had recently left in south London, and he had no regrets about moving home and office to an up-market area in the West End.

The last part of his early-morning walk took him through Crown Passage, a narrow alleyway linking Pall Mall to King Street, which was lined with small shops and sandwich bars. One of the shops sold souvenirs, another was a hardware store, a third repaired shoes and sold umbrellas, and there was a shop which belonged to a dealer in antique and unusual weaponry. Samson sometimes wondered, when he looked at ceremonial swords displayed in the shop window, how much casual trade was attracted by such a specialised service. A notice in the window read:

All sorts of militaria from bygone ages bought and sold. We have a wide selection of antique Samurai swords, armour and helmets in stock. Also available:

7

medieval swords, halberds and helmets, scimitars, poni-
ards, skeans, dirks, *kris, kukris* and *yataghans*. We also
have reduced-size replicas of some items which make
excellent gifts or are eminently collectable.

Sometimes as he passed up Crown Passage Samson would
see a man opening up the premises and they would exchange
tokens of social intercourse like 'Good morning' and 'It
looks like rain today.' This politely meaningless ritual might
have continued indefinitely but one morning the man said,
'Excuse me for asking, but don't you have an office just
round the corner?'
   'I do.'
   'And you are a private investigator?'
   'I am.'
   'I'm thinking of paying you a visit.'
   Samson's heavy-lidded eyes narrowed slightly as he
changed gear from weight-loser to professional gainer. He
took out his wallet and produced a card which he handed
over.
   'This gives my office number and office times,' he said,
and he smiled, revealing a perfect set of small white teeth
embedded like pearls in Schiaparelli pink gums.
   While the other man read the card Samson tried to read
him. He was tall, and spectacles spanned eyes which topped
a long pallid face. His hair was thinning and grey at the
temples, and his dark-grey suit of wool and cashmere looked
tailor-made. A signet ring glittered on the little finger of his
left hand and he wore a Rolex watch on his wrist. His shoes
were black and burnished and Samson sensed a newness
about the man as if he had been kitted out and wasn't really
accustomed to the style or image he was presenting. Perhaps
he had recently come into money or was courting a woman.
   Having read the card with the concentrated calculation
some people give to restaurant bills the man looked up and
said, 'I'll give you a call to arrange an appointment, or
could we fix something now?'

8

'Give me a call. I don't carry a note of my appointments with me, Mr Ruddick.'

The other man raised his eyebrows. 'You know my name?'

'It isn't difficult. You seem to be the owner of this shop – if shop is the right word – and it's called, "Frank Ruddick and Co. Militaria." No great feat of deduction.'

'No, I suppose not.' Ruddick sounded disappointed, as though he'd hoped for a wider form of recognition.

Discerning an air of disappointment Samson said, 'Haven't I heard you on the radio? Your name rings a bell.'

This shot in the dark lightened the other man's face, and he prodded his spectacles so that they sat more firmly on the bridge of his nose.

'No, but I've had an article on collectables published in a colour supplement.'

'That must be it,' said Samson, and then, motioning towards the notice in the window, 'By the way, what is a *yataghan*?'

Ruddick's eyes gleamed with the enthusiasm of an expert who loves to impart information on his special subject. 'It's a curved Turkish sword without a guard or cross-piece. I don't have one in stock at the moment but I have a smaller replica, an accurate representation in every detail, if you would care to see it.'

'Not today, thank you,' said Samson hurriedly. 'I must be on my way.'

Samson's office near St James's Square was staffed by two young women. Both were physically attractive although so far as he was concerned this was merely an incidental bonus. Qualities of loyalty, adaptability and fast imaginative thinking were far more important.

Shandy had long fair hair and might have been cloned from a Garbo lookalike; she had been Samson's professional help-meet for many years. Georgia was pertly pretty and had been with the firm only a few weeks. She was still on six months' trial. Sharp, smart and streetwise as any tough little

9

Cockney sparrow she would reply, to anyone who cared to ask her occupation, 'I'm dogsbody to a great private eye.'

It was Georgia who took Ruddick's call and arranged an appointment for late that afternoon. When he arrived she conducted him to Samson's room, which was insulated from noise by double-glazed windows and had air conditioning. Green velour curtains were draped by the windows. Chairs for clients were leather-upholstered in the same shade of green which harmonised with a beige carpet that had an extravagantly thick pile. Oil paintings of harbour scenes, a bookcase filled with reference books and a cocktail cabinet containing different brands of malt whisky as well as other spirits and liqueurs were the principal furnishings.

An hour-glass stood on Samson's leather-topped yew-wood desk. It measured half-hours and when each new client entered his room he would tip the glass like a taxi driver switching on his meter. At an initial appointment no one was allowed more than half an hour. Time, its measurement and universal significance, had been a hobby and preoccupation for him for almost as long as he could remember. He respected Time as a creator and first force in the way Aristotle considered God to be the Prime Mover of the world and some quantum physicists and other thinkers regard Energy.

He tipped the hour-glass as Ruddick entered the room. And then, rising slowly to his feet, he said, 'Please take a seat, Mr Ruddick. Sit on it, if you wish.'

Ruddick looked faintly surprised but gave a conventional 'Thank you.'

When his client was seated Samson said, 'My services are at your disposal. How can I help?'

'I don't know where to begin.'

'Begin at the end, or with a loose end, if it's easier than beginning at the beginning.'

Ruddick adjusted his spectacles. 'It would indeed be easier to commence at the end,' he said.

Samson had already switched on a tape-recorder hidden

in a desk drawer and linked to the hour-glass, which had a concealed microphone in its base, but he reached for a notepad and ballpoint pen.

'This will sound incredible,' Ruddick went on, 'indeed, it is incredible. I am hoping to marry a lady who is a widow and now, at the eleventh hour, her husband has turned up – alive!'

'Unusual, but not incredible,' said Samson. 'There is a biblical precedent for resurrection. How did this lady's husband die?'

'A motor accident.'

Ruddick paused as if awaiting Samson's reaction. Samson reacted by saying, 'Go on.'

'It was a foggy day and for some unexplained reason he was driving in the country. His car must have gone at some speed into the bottom of a railway bridge which crossed the road. Apparently he suffered ghastly injuries. But during the last fortnight he has turned up whole and well.'

'How long ago was the car crash?'

'Just over two years ago. But now, bold as brass, he's arrived to pester my lady friend at her house. And he seems to want to resume relations with her.' Ruddick leaned forward as if to share a confidence he didn't want to be overheard. It brought him closer to the microphone. 'She, poor dear,' he said, 'doesn't know what to do, and neither do I.'

Samson, who had been toying with the pen, put it down and said, 'You want me to discredit him.'

'I beg your pardon.'

'You want me to find evidence that will discredit this man who has risen from the dead.'

Ruddick shifted nervously in his seat. 'Well, put like that, and in a word, yes.'

Samson picked up his pen. 'What is the name of your lady friend?'

'Mary.'

11

'Mary what?'

'Mary Coomber.'

'And the husband's name?'

'Colin. Colin Coomber.'

Samson wrote down the names. 'How did you come to meet Mrs Coomber?' he asked.

'I don't understand why that should concern you.'

'Don't you want to answer?'

'It's not that I don't wish to answer,' replied Ruddick irritably. 'It's that I don't understand why what is essentially a part of my private life should concern you. But, if you must know, she came into my shop one day with a sword which belonged to an aunt. It was something her aunt's father had picked up during travels in the Middle East. The aunt had been told it had been in the Crusades and Mary wanted to check its value for insurance purposes.'

'Was it a medieval sword?' Samson asked.

'No. The moment she took it out of its protective cover I could see it was Circassian, late seventeenth century, but still of value. Quite a nice piece.' Ruddick's speech had quickened with enthusiasm but it slowed down when he went on, 'But this is a digression. What is far more relevant is that the aunt in question has since died and left Mary, her only beneficiary, a considerable sum of money.'

'Do you think the husband's return is connected with the inheritance?'

'I'm sure of it. He probably read of the death. Obituaries appeared in several newspapers. Like her father, the aunt was a great traveller. She had crossed both the Gobi and Sahara deserts and written books about her travels.'

Samson leaned back in his swivel-chair and half-closed his sleepy eyes. 'So we have this situation,' he said. 'A husband presumed dead has reappeared to the consternation of his widow – "widow" in quotes – who has inherited a lot of money and you, who hope to marry the "widow", suspect his motives. What explanation did the husband give for his resurrection?'

12

'He said he couldn't remember anything of the past from the day he was dismissed from his job. That was on the day of the accident. His mind went a complete blank. And then according to him – and I'm relating what Mary has told me – according to him he was working in a bar in Yorkshire when a fight broke out and someone hit him over the head with a bottle. His memory came back as a result of the blow. That is, it came back with regard to his life up to the time of his dismissal from his job but he still doesn't remember what happened after that, nor why he should have been working in a bar in Yorkshire.'

'Amnesia is such a convenient condition,' remarked Samson. 'Available to anyone and yet genuinely suffered by only a few. He didn't remember a car crash?'

'No. He couldn't understand why anyone should have thought it was him in the car.'

'And why did his wife, Mary, think it was him? I assume she identified him.'

Ruddick shook his head. 'That's the trouble, Mr Samson. She didn't see the body. I've started at the end, as you suggested, perhaps I should now turn to the beginning of this extraordinary business.'

Samson glanced at the hour-glass. Sands were trickling through and had filled a quarter of the lower globe.

'Yes,' he said, 'start at the beginning of the events leading up to the car crash. You mentioned that Mr Coomber had been dismissed from his job. What was the job and why was he sacked?'

'This is very difficult,' said Ruddick uneasily. 'Very difficult indeed. I have no first-hand knowledge. It is hearsay, as it were . . . '

'Does Mrs Coomber know you've come to see me?'

'Heavens, no! I'm doing this entirely off my own bat at the moment. She is a sweet woman who thinks ill of no one and she accepts his extraordinary story. She is easily swayed by any hard-luck story. I am more a man of the world, as

I'm sure you are, and I find the whole business very fishy. Very fishy indeed.'

'Fishy it may be,' said Samson with a hint of weariness in his voice, 'but from your hearsay knowledge what was Mr Coomber's job and why was he sacked?'

'I gather he was a sales representative for a pharmaceutical company which manufactured drugs and so on. Its headquarters were in New York but there was a European branch in Brussels and Coomber was attached to that branch. Incidentally, Mary had no idea he'd been dismissed. That only came out later, which made the shock of his sudden death even greater.'

'Are you saying he concealed it from her?'

'No. The facts, as I understand them, are these. He was dismissed on a Tuesday because his work wasn't up to scratch. He was given a year's salary as a sort of golden handshake. He asked for the money in American dollars, which seems most unusual. Why didn't he accept a cheque? Be that as it may, he returned to England that same day and, according to Mary, must have straight away used some of the dollars in the purchase of a used white Mercedes. It was about six years old. I understand, but bought from a reputable dealer. A body was found in the crashed Mercedes. I should explain that Mary wasn't at home at the time. She was visiting her aunt. She was using her own small car. She had no idea that he was in any trouble, and might be dismissed, and wasn't expecting him back in England until the following week-end. She arrived home to find a police car parked outside her house.'

Ruddick paused, took out a handkerchief, and mopped his brow. 'All this is most unpleasant,' he said. 'I feel like the school sneak. But I'm doing it purely for Mary's protection. I do hope you understand that. I have no wish for any personal gain.'

Samson nodded his head.

'She has such a generous nature,' Ruddick continued,

14

'she is generous to a fault. It would be easy for a man such as Coomber to exploit her generosity.'

'Do you have any evidence that he's doing that?'

'Well, yes. It seems that for some years his hobby had been making video films. I think he was probably more interested in that than in selling tranquillisers and appetite suppressants. Anyway, he is soliciting Mary for a substantial sum with which to set up a company for the production of video films. I gather that there are a number of such independent companies in existence and they sometimes produce films which are purchased by the BBC and ITV and sold to television networks abroad.'

'We'll come back to that in a moment,' said Samson. 'First, tell me about the police car waiting outside her house. Were the police bringing news of the crash?'

'Exactly. A woman police constable accompanied her indoors. She said there had been a serious accident. The driver had been very badly injured and must have died instantly. He hadn't been wearing a seat belt. The police woman produced a wallet which contained driving licence and credit cards and asked if Mary could identify these. She did, and promptly fainted. I believe she was also shown a ring which had been removed from a finger. It was Coomber's. She was asked whether she wished to see the body but was advised that Coomber's face was virtually unrecognisable and it would probably be sufficient that she had identified the wallet and ring. Furthermore, the car had been traced by the police computer as belonging to an employee of the garage which sold Coomber the car. They had issued an insurance cover note in his name and this was in his wallet. In view of all the circumstances Mary didn't think it necessary to go to the mortuary. Oh yes, and there was his suitcase in the back of the car with his clothes and some laundry.'

Ruddick took off his spectacles and wiped them with a fresh handkerchief which he took from his breast pocket. He looked at Samson through squeezed-up eyes. 'It might

15

have been better if she'd tried to make a positive identification,' he went on. 'She didn't even receive his clothes. She asked that they be destroyed. They were in a sorry state, I believe.'

Samson, who had made one or two notes while Ruddick was speaking, put down his pen and said, 'You are suggesting that it wasn't Mr Coomber in the car, but someone else, and someone else has been buried or cremated in error.'

'I think it must be the case.'

'Let me recap,' said Samson after glancing at the hourglass. 'Mr Coomber is sacked in a peremptory way by a company operating in Brussels but is given a year's salary as compensation. His wife knows nothing of this. He returns to England, immediately buys a second-hand Mercedes, and gets involved in a car accident. It seems he has been fatally injured in the accident, but two years later he appears, fit and well, stating that from the moment of dismissal he can remember nothing.'

'That is correct.'

'Have you or Mrs Coomber any idea why he should want his golden handshake in dollars or why he should want to buy a car the moment he returns to England?'

'Well, Mary seems to think he wanted to put a good face on his dismissal and return to her in some style. I'm not so charitable. I think he may have been plotting a disappearing act.'

'Have you met him?' Samson asked.

For a moment Ruddick looked acutely uncomfortable. He lowered his head, shunted about in his chair and plucked at his trouser creases. Before speaking he touched the rim of his spectacles as though adjusting them on the bridge of his nose. It was a nervous mannerism and Samson wondered why the question he had asked should so perturb his visitor.

'I've met him a couple of times. He's called to take Mary out. Not to put too fine a point on it, Mr Samson, I reside with her at her house. I sold my own little property and moved in with her. As I've told you, I was hoping to marry her. But please don't draw the wrong conclusion. I respect Mary and have the old-fashioned idea that one should not live fully as man and wife before marriage. We share the same living quarters but not the same sleeping quarters. I hope that is clear.'

'Quite clear. Has Mrs Coomber informed the authorities that someone has been buried or cremated who was not her husband? Was he buried or cremated?'

'Cremated. No, she hasn't told anyone. The prospect of enquiries appals her, and Coomber has been influencing her. He has advised her to do nothing. I don't feel it is for me . . . ' Ruddick left the sentence unfinished.

'Did she collect insurance money as a result of his supposed death?' Samson asked.

'Not a penny,' Ruddick replied firmly. 'I asked the very same question. If she had, she would have been honour-bound to return it.'

'She must have received something for the crashed car.'

'Possibly. I never asked about that. But, knowing Mary, I very much doubt if she ever put in a claim. As I've said, she's very generous and sometimes doesn't seem to realise the importance of money.'

'I sometimes think,' said Samson reflectively, 'that money is more important than anything except perhaps good health.' The statement was untrue but he wanted to draw Ruddick out, to discover how Ruddick felt about monetary wealth.

'You are so right, Mr Samson. I couldn't agree more.'

Having satisfied himself on Ruddick's attitude to money Samson asked what sort of films Colin Coomber planned to make.

Ruddick sat forward on his seat. 'I'm glad you asked that. When I made the same enquiry of Mary she was uncharacteristically vague but I gather they were to be in some way historical, relating to history, that is.'

'How soon after the car was purchased did the accident occur?'

'How soon? The time interval, you mean?'

'Yes.'

Ruddick had the look on his face of a man scanning the departure times on an airport information board. After a thoughtful pause he said, 'I think he bought the car at about one o'clock on that Tuesday afternoon and the accident occurred at approximately three-thirty the same day. The time of the accident is approximate because there were no witnesses. It was a day of patchy fog and the car was obviously going too fast for the weather conditions. Someone who was walking a dog found the crashed car and reported it at once to the police.'

'No witnesses. A story of amnesia partially cured. I'm inclined to agree with you, Mr Ruddick. It is fishy. I imagine you want me to find out exactly what happened in the hope of discrediting Mr Coomber in the eyes of his wife, the woman you hope to marry. Am I right?'

Although Ruddick had replaced his spectacles after vigorous cleaning he didn't look directly at Samson when he replied, 'You put it very bluntly, but yes.' He fingered the rim of the spectacles and then went on, 'I don't like going behind Mary's back. She is honest with me. I feel I'm deceiving her.'

Samson gave a faint smile. 'If you had been in my trade or profession for as long as I you would realise that most of our lives are spent in deceptions of one sort or another, and that self-deception is the most common of all deceptions.'

'I'm not sure . . . Do you mean that I . . . '

Samson raised his hand as though to prevent any sort of disclaimer. 'I accept that what you are doing is for Mrs Coomber's protection. Not that this is any of my business. I'm simply a hired gumshoe. So, let's get down to practicalities. I have to tell you that my fees are high. I'm reputed to be the most expensive investigator in London.'

'How much?'

The question, fired like a bullet, was completely different from his normal mannered and rather pedantic speech.

18

'Usually,' said Samson, 'I charge by the hour and add expenses. In this case I would charge seventy pounds an hour plus expenses but I feel in a gambling mood today and, if you prefer, I'll quote you a figure for professional fees and expenses all inclusive.'

'Seventy pounds an hour! That's absurd!'

'Take it or leave it,' said Samson casually, 'or take my alternative offer.'

'All right. What is your all-in figure?'

'Three and a half thousand.'

'Three and a half thousand pounds! That's ridiculous! You might get all the information you need in a single day.'

'Or it might take weeks. Look at it like this. For what you want I'm charging you the price you'd charge for a very rare sword. For example, the sword used by Lord Raglan when leading the charge of the Light Brigade.'

'I'm not aware of the existence of that sword and if it came up for auction I'd expect it to reach more than three and a half.'

'That makes my point surely. Aren't my services worth more than an old steel blade? And bear in mind that my expenses could be enormous. Suppose, for example, that during his so-called amnesia Mr Coomber had been to Australia and I was obliged to pursue enquiries there. The expenses would be enormous but these wouldn't be charged if you accept my all-in figure. With the three and a half thousand deal there would be no payment without a satisfactory result, and by satisfactory result I mean obtaining evidence that Mr Coomber never had amnesia and returned to his wife simply to improve his finances. Wouldn't that be a satisfactory outcome?'

Ruddick thought for a moment. 'Well, yes,' he said. 'But I still think your charges are exorbitant.' He stood up. 'I feel sure I could get the same service at a much more reasonable figure elsewhere.'

Samson slowly shook his head. 'I doubt it. Cheaper, yes.

But I will guarantee that you get the required result and no one else would do that.'

'You are extremely confident.'

Samson gave a self-depreciating smile. 'I have reason to be.'

'All the same, Mr Samson, I'm not prepared to engage your services and, to be perfectly frank, I can't understand how you remain in business with such inflated charges.'

Samson looked at the hour-glass. The sands had not yet quite run out. 'I don't charge for initial consultations of less than half an hour,' he said magnanimously. 'There will be no charge for today's consultation. Good afternoon, Mr Ruddick.'

2

The following day Samson went for his customary walk round the park. It was a fine morning in May. Daffodils were fading but banks of red and yellow tulips were in full bloom. Although early, tourists were already standing on the bridge feeding sparrows and taking photographs. An American woman stopped him. 'Pardon me,' she said, 'but can you tell me if the Queen is in residence?' As she spoke she glanced across the lake at the squat outline of Buckingham Palace.

Samson had no idea of the monarch's whereabouts. He couldn't see any flag but didn't want to disappoint an earnest contributor to the nation's invisible earnings. 'I am sure she is in residence,' he said. This can't be altogether untrue, he thought, she must be in residence somewhere. He smiled and went on his way.

Walking up Crown Passage he spotted a familiar figure. It was Ruddick and he seemed to be waiting for someone. As he drew nearer Samson realised Ruddick was waiting for him.

'Good morning, Mr Samson . . . Mr Samson?'

'Yes?'

Ruddick lowered his voice as though afraid of being overheard by pedestrians hurrying by and said, 'I have been reconsidering the matter. I am willing to accept your terms. Three and a half, all inclusive.'

'How wise.'

'Er, could you see me today?'

'A meeting could be arranged. But it'll probably have to be early evening. I know I've got a full day ahead.'

'Any time you say.'

'Then give my office a call. By the way, do you know if Her Majesty is in residence at the palace?'

'I don't think she is. I believe she's at Windsor.'

'How inconsiderate of her,' said Samson.

Leaving Ruddick looking mystified, Samson moved on.

His staff of two were accustomed to working overtime and it was no surprise to Georgia to be told that, if Ruddick telephoned, six in the evening would be convenient for an appointment. 'I hope that staying on late won't put out any of your arrangements,' said Samson considerately.

'No, it doesn't matter. I haven't got no boyfriend at the moment.'

'Any boyfriend,' Samson corrected.

'Sorry. Slip of the tongue.'

Samson patted her shoulder. 'You're doing very well, Georgia.'

'Thanks. I like it here.'

Promptly at six she called on the intercom to say that Ruddick had arrived.

'Keep him waiting ten minutes,' said Samson, 'and then bring him up.'

'Will do.'

When Ruddick was shown into Samson's room after the allotted time he seemed tense and he walked with a slight limp.

'Thank you for seeing me at this rather late hour, Mr Samson. I trust I'm not keeping you.'

'No one has ever before suggested I might be a kept man,' replied Samson with a smile. 'Do sit down. I won't ask what the problem is. I already know that. But I'm curious to know why you changed your mind about my services.'

Ruddick suddenly looked like a man about to burst, and he burst out, 'She's seeing him tomorrow night.'

'And you disapprove.'

'I most certainly do. I'm convinced he's after her money and she is behaving like a gullible child. We discussed – well, we argued about – it last night. She is seeing too much of him for her own good, Mr Samson.'

'He *is* her husband,' said Samson quietly.

'Yes, indeed he is. And in the normal course I would do the decent thing and fade from the picture but I'm convinced that he never had amnesia and that he's only come back to milk her of her inheritance.'

'Did she say why she wanted to see him?' Samson asked.

'She said she felt sorry for him and, like you, she pointed out he was her husband. She is a very loyal woman, too loyal for her own good.'

'But you want her to be loyal to you,' said Samson.

'There is loyalty and loyalty. True loyalty and misguided loyalty. I'm sorry to have to say it, but her loyalty to him is misguided.'

'Let's not commit the folly of self-deception,' said Samson, 'you are not at all sorry. What you want is for me to produce evidence that Mrs Coomber's loyalty really is misguided. Am I right?'

'Not to mince words, yes.'

The tape-recorder was running but Samson picked up his pen. He had found that clients became inhibited if they knew their words were being taped but were somehow reassured when they saw him making notes.

'I'd like some more information,' he said. 'Yesterday you told me you had moved in with Mrs Coomber. That is the address we have for you?'

'It is.'

'And at what time tomorrow is she meeting her husband?'

'He's calling at seven.'

Samson scribbled the time on his notepad.

'Why is she meeting him?'

'I wish I knew. She's told me she cares for me, cares deeply, and yet she's meeting him. Before he arrived, out

23

of the blue, she had told me many times he had made her unhappy during their married life. He is a womaniser, Mr Samson. And, in my opinion, a conman.'

'Do you know where he lives?'

'I believe he is staying at a hotel in the Russell Square area and that surprises me slightly.'

'Why?'

'Well, according to Mary, he always wanted the very best. The best hotels, the best places in a restaurant, the best clothes. He believed in appearances. Façades. On his income it meant he was almost permanently in debt. He had a dozen credit cards and probably as many bank accounts. He was a classic case of someone living beyond his means. I don't know how Mary could have put up with it.'

Samson, pen poised, said, 'There are some reasonably good hotels in the Russell Square area.'

'Maybe, but it's not Park Lane.'

'Do you know the name of the hotel?'

'No. I asked Mary, but she doesn't know either.'

'If all his credit cards were found on a body after the car crash, and if he has had amnesia, or has wanted to escape from creditors, it may not be surprising that he isn't slumming at the Dorchester. On the other hand, he did have a golden handshake. Under what name is he registered at the hotel?'

'I don't know that either.' Ruddick fidgeted on his chair. 'I'm only repeating what I gleaned from Mary.'

'Can you tell me the exact date of the car crash?'

'It was just over two years ago. The twenty-second of March.'

Samson made a note of the date.

'And the name of the firm that sold him the Mercedes?' he asked.

'Maurice Moxon Motors at Whetstone, I believe.'

'The name of the company he worked for in Brussels?'

'Semco Incorporated.'

While Samson made written notes he mentally noted

24

the promptness of Ruddick's replies. There had been no hesitations. Most known facts about his rival were evidently at the top of Ruddick's mind.

'How much else can you tell me about Mr Coomber?' he asked.

The moment he had spoken he knew it was the wrong question. If Ruddick had been a tortoise his head would have retreated into its carapace; if he had been a bird he would have flown.

'I only know what Mary has told me,' Ruddick said. 'It's all hearsay.'

'Can you tell me which police authority was involved when the accident was discovered, and where the inquest was held?'

'I'm sorry. I don't know.'

'I can find out,' said Samson.

'You won't add the cost to your bill,' Ruddick asked sharply.

Samson gave his widest pearls-in-pink-coral smile. 'Of course not. The three and a half thousand includes all incidentals and disbursements.'

Ruddick gave a brief smirk of satisfaction.

To show that he had temporarily finished taking notes Samson ostentatiously put down his pen. 'In my job,' he said, 'it is sometimes necessary to ask personal questions but all answers are treated with absolute confidentiality.'

He paused and awaited Ruddick's reaction.

'I understand that. What do you want to know?'

'You've told me that you had something of an argument with Mrs Coomber last night. What was the argument about?'

'I thought I'd made that obvious. I much resent the intrusion of that man into our lives. Mary was quite happy until his appearance. Now she's at sixes and sevens. You ask what the argument was about. I think he should be given his marching orders but she's too sensitive to the feelings of others to take a tough line. All right, I accept that she can't be hard, but I do think that if she must see him it should be in my presence. I don't like them meeting on their own. But, in her gentle way, she can be quite strong-willed, and she insists on the two of them discussing the future on their own. It was at this point she sprung it on me that he had phoned her during the day and she had agreed to go out with him tomorrow night. She had obviously given him her telephone number, *our* telephone number.'

The effort of this explanation left Ruddick slightly breathless and flushed. His eyes glinted angrily.

Samson picked up his pen. 'Do you know where they intend going?'

'I've no idea. He'll take her for a meal somewhere, I suppose.' Ruddick paused and a bitter note entered his voice as he added, 'She said she'd leave something for me in the microwave if I'm not home when she leaves.'

'Useful gadgets, microwave ovens,' said Samson, affecting not to notice the change of tone. 'Now then, I'd like to know his age, your age and hers.'

Ruddick's posture changed. He sat stiffly upright in his chair. 'I don't understand the relevance of that,' he said.

Samson ignored the comment. 'How old is Mr Coomber?'

'If you must know, he is thirty-nine.'

'And you?'

For a few moments it seemed that Ruddick wasn't going to reply but eventually he muttered, 'Fifty.'

'And Mrs Coomber?'

'She's the same age as him. A few months younger.'

'I'd like a photograph of him. Do you have one?'

'I do not. Mary had a photograph on top of the television set when I first came to live in her house. But it has disappeared and recently she's put a photo of the two of us, taken while on holiday in Majorca, in its place.'

'Can you provide me with a photo?'

'I suppose I could, yes.'

'There must be items belonging to him around the house

as it's only two years since his presumed death. Clothes, keepsakes, oddments of some sort or another.'

Ruddick shook his head. 'She sold the house they'd owned as joint tenants and moved out of the district where they'd lived. I believe she disposed of nearly everything.'

'I know you both live in her house at Woodford Green in Essex but where did she live with Mr Coomber?'

'In Temple Fortune. That's a district of north London close to Golders Green.'

Without looking at his client, and busily engaged in writing, Samson asked, 'How did Mr Coomber trace her to Woodford Green?'

'I asked exactly the same question. I said, "How the devil did he find you?" and she said he had called at the Temple Fortune house and the new owners had given him Mary's address. She'd given it to them so that they could forward on any mail.'

'I see. Can you tell me how long the Coombers have been married?'

Ruddick winced at the collective name. 'About nine or ten years, I believe.'

'Do you know anything of Mr Coomber's antecedents? What he did and how he lived before marriage? Anything about his childhood?'

Ruddick didn't answer immediately. He gazed at the signet ring on his little finger as though it were a miniaturised memory-bank and then said, 'I know hardly anything. Mary hasn't told me much. I gather he has always been a philanderer and, in my opinion, a whiner. The world has been against him. Unhappy at school. That sort of thing. Well, we can all make out we've had raw deals.' He looked directly at Samson. 'I'm pretty sure my childhood was unhappier than his, I can tell you that.'

The information was of little interest to Samson, who then asked if the marriage had produced any children.

'No!' The negative was explosive. In a more measured voice Ruddick continued, 'It was just as well there were no children to look after when he disappeared. Mary was left facing a pile of debts. If it hadn't been for financial help from her aunt I don't know how she would have coped with the situation.'

At some points during the interview Ruddick had spoken in short, staccato sentences but he had now reverted to what seemed his normal mode of speech. When the tape was played back Samson knew he would be able to identify those parts where Ruddick had appeared to be under stress. He put down his pen and sat back.

'I think that's all for the present, Mr Ruddick. I'll be in touch.'

'Have you any ideas yet?'

'I have no ideas, no theories, at present. But I shall have.'

Samson stood up to emphasise that the interview was at an end. Ruddick also rose to his feet and as he moved forward a spasm of pain crossed his face. 'I twisted my ankle last night,' he said. 'Some fool drove at me. If I could have got the car's number I'd have reported it. I expect the fellow was drunk.'

'Deliberately drove at you?' Samson asked. 'What exactly happened?'

'Well, I'd gone across the road to an off-licence. We were out of Martini and Mary likes a dry Martini as an aperitif. On my way back the road was clear except for a parked car which had its hazard warning lights blinking. Someone had presumably broken down. I was just crossing the road when this car started up and drove straight at me. In jumping clear I twisted my ankle. Obviously the fool hadn't seen me. The street lighting isn't too good at that part. I shall be making a complaint about the lighting to the local authority.'

'You didn't get the make of the car?'

'No. Nor its number.'

'A pity.'

'I entirely agree. People like that shouldn't be loose on the roads. And when they are caught for dangerous or drunken driving the magistrates are far too lenient. I would penalise them heavily. Really punish them. We live in an age where there is too much crime and too little punishment.'

'And too much intolerance and too little compassion. Good evening, Mr Ruddick.'

Shandy was getting ready to leave when Samson walked into her room. In his hand was the tape of the interview with Ruddick.

'I'm not doing that tonight,' she said. 'I'm late already, and Paul is taking me out to dinner.'

Samson placed the cassette on her desk next to a covered typewriter. 'I wouldn't dream of detaining you. Give Paul my regards. By the way, are you free tomorrow night?'

Shandy flicked back a loose lock of blonde hair which had fallen over her forehead. She gave her employer a penetrating look. 'Why do you ask? Do you want to take me out to dinner too?'

'Not this time. Another time perhaps. It's a tail job. I need a co-driver.'

Shandy glanced at her watch and put down her handbag. 'I can manage two minutes. What's the job?'

'I'll explain in more detail tomorrow. But I want to follow a man when he collects a woman to take her out for the evening. Because he is temporarily resident at a hotel in or near Russell Square I'd guess he won't have a car but will arrive in a hired car or taxi. If I'm on my own that can make tailing difficult. People can hop out at traffic lights and get lost in a crowd while I'm stuck looking for somewhere to park. But if I've got a co-driver . . . '

'She can take over while you hop out,' Shandy took over for him.

'Exactly.'

She picked up her handbag. 'All right. You're on. It's a good thing I've got an understanding husband.'

'But it's also a good thing, so far as I'm concerned, that not every husband is an understanding man,' said Samson.

'Too much understanding between the sexes could seriously damage the interests of my noble profession.'

It was a few minutes before seven on the following evening when Samson parked his car, a specially equipped Ford Granada, in a slip road from where he could view a block of four town houses with Georgian façades. Beyond the terrace of houses was a large garage forecourt with access to a dual carriageway.

'I hope Coomber or his driver doesn't park next to us,' said Samson after he and Shandy had changed seats.

'If he does, we shall have to use the illicit-lovers routine . . . Don't look so apprehensive,' she laughed.

'I'm not apprehensive of giving you an affectionate embrace for the purpose of hiding our faces.'

'No? But you might have put it more gallantly.'

'Anyway, the situation probably won't arise.'

'He said hopefully.'

Samson shook his head and remained silent. It wasn't that he was lost for words but he had learned from experience that when it came to teasing word-play Shandy invariably won.

After a pause she said, 'Mary Coomber must be quite an attractive woman. Two men after her.'

'Money has its place among the aphrodisiacs,' remarked Samson, 'and she has money.'

'You are so unromantic!'

'Romance and realism are incompatible,' said Samson. 'Show me a romantic and . . . ' He broke off. 'I think a romantic has just arrived.'

A blue BMW had come to a halt and parked in a space reserved for buses in front of the town houses. Almost at once the car's hazard lights began blinking.

3

A fair-haired man wearing a blue blazer and light-grey slacks jumped out of the passenger door. Moving with athletic grace he ran across the pavement, vaulted a small gate, crossed a tiny front garden and bounded up three steps. He came to a stop with his hand pressed against a door-bell.

'Can't really tell from here,' said Shandy, 'but he seems a good-looker. Knocks spots off Ruddick in that department.'

'I didn't know you'd seen Ruddick.'

'I saw him in the waiting room and asked Georgia who he was.'

The front door opened and a woman stepped out. It wasn't easy to distinguish individual features at a distance but she had short, dark, swept-back hair, clearly defined eyebrows, and her face seemed flushed. She was slender and wore a navy-blue and white two-piece suit. The man who had called for her and who was, the watchers presumed, Colin Coomber, opened the car's rear door. She stepped inside and he followed. It was then evident that introductions were being made because the driver turned in his seat, reached back and shook hands with the woman.

'Not a hired chauffeur,' Samson observed. 'That was a social introduction. Get ready to go.'

Shandy switched on the engine and was about to move out when she noticed the reflection of another car in the wing mirror. She waited, allowing it to pass. The driver, a man, was staring fixedly ahead.

'That,' said Samson, 'looked remarkably like our client.'

'I thought the same. Do you think he saw us?'

'Maybe. Depends on where he was parked.'

Hazard warning lights had been switched off and the blue BMW eased forward making its entry into the stream of traffic travelling south in the direction of the City of London. Ruddick, driving a large red Volvo, slotted his car into the stream. Shandy, in the Granada, had to allow four cars to pass before she could make an entry.

'I wonder if Mrs Coomber realises she is being followed by her live-in man friend,' said Shandy.

'I doubt it. Let's hope neither of the drivers realise there's a third following them both.'

It was a tortuous drive through congested traffic and twice they thought they had lost their quarry. After about half an hour they were travelling along the north side of Regents Park along Prince Albert Road. Samson was unsighted as Shandy suddenly braked sharply.

'The BMW has just turned right,' she said.

'What about the Volvo?'

'It's waiting for a break in the traffic before it can cross . . . Wait a sec. There he goes.'

Samson sighed. 'It's always so much easier to tail on foot.'

As he spoke Shandy took a chance and swung across an oncoming car to be fiercely reproved by a blast from its horn.

'Well done,' said Samson.

A few seconds later Shandy said, 'I think I've lost them.'

'Keep cruising round.'

Shandy drove round a block containing multi-storeyed buildings which were mainly occupied as rented apartments. It was on a third tour of the densely built-up area that she spotted the parked BMW. 'There it is,' she exclaimed, 'but there's no sign of Ruddick's Volvo. Maybe he's lost them.'

'Pull into the side. They've either gone into one of

the flats or they're dining at the Oslo Court restaurant.'

'What are you going to do?'

'Take a chance on the restaurant.'

'With me?'

He shook his head. 'Park just down there.' He indicated a vacant space. 'Then you can go on home. I don't think the trio are going to split up.' He reached for his wallet and took out a twenty-pound note. 'Have this. It'll pay for a taxi to take you home.'

'It won't cost twenty pounds to get to Streatham.'

'Buy some tights with the change. You and Georgia are always moaning about the number of tights you get through.'

Shandy took the note, handed him the car keys and said, 'Good luck. See you tomorrow.'

After locking up the car Samson walked to the next street. Although he had a large frame his legs were short, and he took short steps. This gave the illusion of moving swiftly and purposefully, which was an advantage when pavements were crowded as other pedestrians tended to give way. A party of five people coming from the opposite direction parted and he cleaved through like a battleship scattering corvettes.

As he rounded the street corner he saw the parked red Volvo. He crossed the road and approached from the rear of the car. When he reached it he walked on tip-toe along the side and rapped the driver's window. Ruddick, who hadn't seen him coming, jerked in his seat as though he'd received an electric shock. Recognition of Samson spread from his eyes to his mouth, which sagged open. He wound down the window.

'What are you doing here?' he asked.

'I'm doing my job.'

'You must have followed me.'

'I followed both of you.'

'They've gone into Oslo Court.'

'Yes, I know,' replied Samson in an approximation of the truth. 'Did they see you?'

'No. Who is the fellow with them?'

'That is something I shall find out. Now then, do we really want a duplication of effort? Why don't you go home. We professional bloodhounds have a saying, "Why keep a dog and bark yourself?" Let me do the barking, Mr Ruddick. I'm good at it and my bite is as sharp as my bark.'

Ruddick thought for a moment. 'All right. But I don't want Mary to come to any harm. It's her I'm thinking of. That's the only reason I'm here. I'll go, but I'll expect you to make sure Mary returns safely.'

'Good night, Mr Ruddick.'

As Samson walked away he heard the Volvo's engine start. He recrossed the road and made for the restaurant at Olso Court.

It was a popular eating place but by using a few gracious words in Spanish, and because he had dined there before and was recognised as a good customer, he secured a corner table which was discreetly distant from the table where Mary Coomber and her two escorts were studying the menu.

The colour theme of the restaurant was pink. The linen tablecloth was pink and a pink rose was the centre-piece of his table. Air-conditioning ducts set in low ceilings kept the place cool on what was an exceptionally warm evening. Samson decided to forget that he had been advised by his doctor and Shandy to lose weight and considered it would be appropriate, in view of Ruddick's description of Coomber's story as fishy, to order fish. He settled for crab à la Rochelle followed by salmon *en croute*.

The man who Samson assumed was Colin Coomber had given an order for food and wine and now seemed to be explaining the contents of a sheaf of papers which he had produced. The other man, older and with a long saturnine face below a bald scalp, said little but constantly nodded his head as if in agreement with what Coomber was saying.

When the waiter brought his crab dish Samson said,

'Those three people over at the far end. Isn't the fair-haired man a movie star?'

The waiter turned and looked. 'I don't know, sir.'

'I'll swear I've seen him before. Does he come here often?'

The waiter shrugged. 'I don't think so, although I have seen him once or twice in the last week or two.'

'I think he starred in *The Octopus Has Nine Legs*,' said Samson. 'Very good film. Have you seen it?'

The waiter shook his head.

Samson lowered his voice. 'See if you can find out who he is and who he's with, and let me know. But I don't want them to know I'm enquiring. People in show business are sensitive about their privacy.'

'Very good, sir.'

From time to time during the meal he noticed the waiter hovering near the trio. It was as he was being served a fruit salad from the dessert trolley that the waiter said, 'The gentleman booked the table under the name of Coomber, sir. He may be a movie star, I don't know. But they are talking all the time about making films . . . Cream, sir?'

'No, thank you.'

The waiter put a bowl of fresh fruit salad in front of Samson with the reverence of a priest placing a chalice on an altar.

'You don't know who the bald-headed man is?' enquired Samson.

'No, sir, but I did hear him say he'd set up many package deals.' The waiter's brow became furrowed and he repeated 'package deals' as though the term belonged to some foreign jargon.

Samson slipped a banknote into his hand which was pocketed with the sleight of hand of a conjuror. 'Thank you very much, sir. Coffee?'

'No, I'll have the bill, please.'

He left the restaurant unobserved by the three diners he had been watching. This wasn't difficult; they seemed deep in conversation and the place was crowded with other diners. On returning to his car he drove to the end of the street where the BMW was parked, switched off the engine and waited.

Within half an hour he saw them arrive. The other man held open the door while Coomber assisted his wife into the car, solicitously holding her arm as if to protect her from accidentally brushing against the door panel. Samson suspected that the lingering hold on her arm was an excuse to make physical contact masquerading as chivalrous behaviour. Male gallantry to the female, he reflected, often increased in proportion to the favour desired of the female.

He trailed the BMW to Woodford Green and watched as Coomber with a politeness which almost amounted to parody helped his wife dismount from the car. He was rewarded with a peck on the cheek before she hurried towards the front door of her house. Coomber didn't wait to see her enter. He climbed in beside the driver and the BMW moved away.

Continuing the tail Samson followed the other car back towards the West End. It was as they were travelling down Southampton Row that the BMW suddenly pulled into the kerb. Samson did the same, narrowly missing a jay-walker. He saw Coomber alight from the car, give a salute to the driver and walk away. He leaped out of his car and followed.

Threading his way through pedestrians who seemed to be aimlessly wandering along the pavement he tracked Coomber to the Excelsior Hotel just off Russell Square. Passing through wide plate-glass doors a few paces behind his quarry he entered a reception area which was busy with an influx of newly arrived tourists many of whom had hand-baggage embellished with maple-leaf emblems. Mingling with a party of Canadians he was able to remain unobserved by Coomber as he asked for the key to Room 535.

Satisfied with his evening's work, and with the meal he'd consumed, Samson returned to his car. Within twenty minutes he was in his apartment easing his bulk into a capacious armchair with a glass of whisky strategically placed within easy reach.

For a few moments he reflected on the emotional aspect of the situation involving Colin and Mary Coomber and his client. Sexual rivalry had occurred in many of his cases throughout the years and although he found it difficult to understand why two men should be in contest for a woman he was convinced that he'd come across another example of what was immutable for all time, or for at least as long as humanity survived – the eternal triangle. Experience and instinct told him that unless he could deliver the goods his client would be the first side of the triangle to cave in and allow the other two sides to close and merge.

The following morning when he walked up Crown Passage he was surprised to see that Ruddick's shop was closed and there was no sign of the owner.

When Shandy arrived at the office he told her of the previous evening's events. 'I'd like to know if Coomber is using his own name at the hotel,' he said. 'That could be a little job for Georgia. Ask her to find out. And if she wants to know how, tell her to use her initiative.'

'You're giving her an initiative test.'

'Yes.'

'Right. Will do.'

Within ten minutes Georgia came to his room, her eyes shining with triumph. 'I done it,' she said. 'I used my initiative.'

'And?'

'He's registered as Coomber.'

'Good.'

'Want to know how I did it?'

'Tell me.'

'Well, we knew the room number was 535 and so I rang the hotel, after looking up its number in Yellow Pages, and asked for Room 535. The op put me through and when a man answered I said, "Is that Mr Coomber?"

He said, "Yes." I said, "Would you please hold on. I have a long-distance call for you." And then I made a clicking noise and some hisses and hung up.'

'Leaving him to wonder who wanted him,' said Samson.

'That's right, but does it matter?'

'No. You did well.'

'I'm trying hard.'

'You are. Thanks.'

Samson resumed working on a report on security measures necessary to safeguard a complex of warehouses. He was reaching the end of the report when Georgia rang through to say that Mr Ruddick had called without an appointment but wanted to see him urgently.

'Tell him I'll be free in about five minutes,' said Samson. 'I'll let you know when I'm ready.'

He completed the report but owing to interruptions it was nearly half an hour before he called Georgia to say, 'I can see Mr Ruddick now. Apologise for the delay and show him up. Bring his file with you.'

Flush spots stood out on Ruddick's pale cheeks and he looked agitated as he entered. Georgia, a step behind him, carried a slim folder which she deposited on Samson's desk. As she put it down she gave a meaningful look. It was a mute message that their client wasn't in the best of tempers.

When the door had closed behind her Ruddick moved his chair so that he was directly opposite Samson and within touching distance of the desk. It was a confrontational gesture.

'You said you'd see me in five minutes,' he accused.

'Hasn't my receptionist apologised for the delay?'

'I have business to attend to and . . . '

'Forgive me for interrupting,' said Samson loudly, overriding the other's voice, 'but if you had made an appointment you would have been seen on time. I am punctiliously punctual in such matters. But you didn't make an appointment, and I too have a business to attend to.' He lowered the decibels. 'Now, what can I do for you?'

38

Ruddick breathed in and out heavily before speaking. 'Did you see how they parted last night?'

'Mr and Mrs Coomber?'

'Yes. Mr and Mrs Coomber! . . . Did you see?'

'He assisted her from the car in a most gentlemanly way, she gave him a light peck on the cheek and she went into her house.'

'Exactly. She kissed him!'

'You were watching?'

'Naturally. I was waiting and watching for her return. I was worried for her, as you know. I saw it from an upper window. As she kissed him he gripped her hand. Did you notice that?'

'I can't say I did.'

'No one can tell me he isn't after her. I know his sort. Lustful.'

'They are still husband and wife,' Samson remarked.

'Only because he's turned up in time to stop any chance I have of marrying her. It isn't as though they were separated or divorced. He was supposed to be dead. The marriage finished. It's only a technicality that they are still husband and wife.'

'A fairly important technicality.'

Ruddick's eyes sparked angrily. 'Mr Samson, are you on my side or not?'

'It's not a question of sides,' said Samson smoothly. 'I provide an investigative service, not a support group. I'm not concerned with emotional dilemmas. You are naturally chagrined that the husband of the woman you had hoped to marry has risen from the dead, but that is your problem. My problem is finding out what happened during his so-called amnesia and whether it was a genuine loss of memory, and whether he is simply a conman trying to milk money.'

Ruddick tipped his spectacles on to the bridge of his nose. 'Very well. What progress have you made?'

'Coomber is staying at the Excelsior Hotel, which is fairly near Russell Square underground station. At the restaurant he, his wife and the other man appeared to be discussing film production while having a meal.'

'Who is the other man?'

'I shall find out in due course. I believe he may be an agent of some sort. A fixer. Someone who can put a film package together.'

Ruddick shook his head. 'That's what bothers me. Mary is fishing in waters she doesn't understand. She is so trusting. An innocent. She seems to have forgotten what he was like during their married life. Numerous infidelities. Always in debt. Selfish. Totally inconsiderate of her feelings.'

'I don't see how she could have forgotten. She was your source of information about him, wasn't she?'

'Yes, but all that was before he came back into her life. She seems to view him differently now.'

Flush spots had returned to Ruddick's cheeks and burned like two blotchy red shadows thrown by his glasses.

'She is obviously a forgiving lady,' commented Samson.

'Misplaced forgiveness. I told her as much last night.' Ruddick took off his spectacles and rubbed his eyes. 'We didn't get much sleep, I can tell you. And when I did get to my bed I overslept. I was late at the shop this morning. Mary was very contrite. She felt it was her fault. But it wasn't really her fault. I kept her talking. I was trying to get it through to her that he was exploiting her.'

'And did you get it through?' asked Samson, his curiosity getting the better of his claim that he wasn't concerned with emotional dilemmas but simply with providing an investigative service.

'No. She has a stubborn streak. Gently stubborn. It beats me. To anyone else it would be patently obvious that he's after her money.' Almost under his breath he added, 'And her body.'

Samson saw no reason to prolong the interview. Ruddick had simply called to see what, if anything, had been discovered the previous evening, and to vent his jealous anxieties.

40

'Leave everything to me, Mr Ruddick. I'll be in touch when I have something firm to report.'

'There is one other thing.'

'Yes.'

'The type of video they propose to make. Frankly it wouldn't surprise me if these were of the pornographic variety but of course they didn't tell Mary that. What do you think they told her?'

'I've no idea,' said Samson, his eyes almost closed as though he was about to drop off to sleep.

'Educational! Colin isn't interested in education.'

Samson's eyes opened fractionally. 'Colin?'

'Mary always refers to him as Colin and I must have picked up the habit.' Momentarily Ruddick seemed disconcerted, then he continued, 'The main film project is supposedly concerned with classical myths and the relationship between Love and War. Venus and Mars. I imagine that gives it an educational gloss. The end product will probably be nothing more than a sex and violence film, and I've told Mary as much. But she is so trusting. She's even suggested that for the war part they might obtain some props from me. She thought it would somehow be good publicity for me to have my name on the credits. As if I'd want to be connected in any way with that man!' Ruddick's voice quivered with indignation. After a pause, and in a quieter tone, he went on, 'She was thinking of me, of course, and not considering the wider issue, that it would mean bringing Coomber and me together as colleagues.' He peered at Samson. 'It looks as though you might have had as little sleep as I.'

Samson yawned. 'Possibly.'

'I must be on my way.' Ruddick stood up and placed an envelope on the desk. 'You wanted a photo of him. You'll find one in that. You're welcome to it.'

41

4

It was one-fifteen in the afternoon when Samson entered the Excelsior Hotel and drifted towards the reception desk. In his opinion one of the best times to break into a hotel room was when the guest was likely to be having a meal elsewhere, although there was always the hazard of being discovered by hotel staff employed to change bed linen and towelling.

He noticed that the key for Room 535 was hanging on a hook. This probably meant Coomber was not in his room but, to make doubly sure, he went to a phone booth in the hotel and made a call. He asked for Room 535. After a pause the operator said, 'I'm not getting an answer.' Samson thanked her and rang off.

He made his way by lift to the fifth floor and walked along a corridor at the end of which was a trolley piled with used linen. There was no chambermaid in sight, but from within the room came the sound of a woman's voice. Samson listened intently. Each word came clearly through the locked door and he soon realised that he was hearing an early-afternoon newscast. Either someone inside the room was almost stone deaf or the TV had been switched on to give the impression that the room was occupied.

There had been no indication at the restaurant that Coomber was hard of hearing. Samson opened his briefcase and took out what Shandy referred to as his latest toy, an American invention known as a key gun which could open most locks simply by being pressed against them. It resembled a revolver and had a mechanical tool in its barrel. After checking that the corridor was still empty Samson operated the key gun. A moment later he turned the door handle and entered the room.

It was typical of many single-bedded hotel rooms. There was a built-in wardrobe, a washbasin with mirror above, a built-in dressing table with drawers beside the washbasin, and a chair. The colour television set in one corner could be viewed from the bed and at that moment was showing a weather forecast.

Samson reached into his briefcase, took out thin surgical rubber gloves and slipped them on his hands. He was now ready to search the room. Ignoring toothbrush, toothpaste and electric razor by the washbasin, and a half-full bottle of brandy on the dressing table, he went straight to the adjoining drawers. Most of these were empty but one contained a couple of pairs of underpants and some socks. A single drawer in a small bedside table contained a copy of Gideon's Bible and a packet of contraceptives.

Samson went to the wardrobe. Two shirts and a blue blazer which he recognised as having seen the previous evening hung at the end of a bar on which there were several unused clothes-hangers. After closing the wardrobe door he went to a suitcase which lay on the floor beside the bed. He stooped down and pressed the hasps, but the case was locked. Once more he used the key gun but this time it was ineffective and he knew it would be necessary to use old-fashioned methods. Taking a bunch of skeleton keys from his briefcase he began working on the locks and soon was able to lift the lid.

He went quickly through the contents of the suitcase taking care not to disturb their relative positions. He found a box of tissues, a blue tie with a fox-head motif, a paperback thriller, a packet of paracetamol, a girlie magazine, a video camera, some video cassettes, a video magazine, an envelope postmarked 'Bath', a pink file marked 'Video Projects' and a passport.

He took out the passport and opened it. The bearer was named as Colin Charles Coomber. The photograph showed head and shoulders of a fair-haired man, mouth down-drawn at one corner and upturned at the other. It was recognisably Coomber but not so flattering as the one provided by Ruddick. Descriptive details on the passport gave his occupation as salesman and his place of birth as Bristol. Samson flicked through the pages. These bore stamps showing entries to Belgium, France, Italy and Spain, but were of little interest as they were all dated prior to Coomber's disappearance.

After replacing the passport Samson examined the pink file. It contained half a dozen pages covered with handwritten notes and columns of figures headed 'Provisional Budget'. Inside an envelope marked 'Star Quality' were glossy photographs of different women in various stages of undress. Samson wasn't interested in the women but he wanted to know what the notes concerned. He took a small camera from the briefcase and rapidly photographed the written contents of the file. Next he picked up the envelope which was postmarked 'Bath' and addressed to Mr Colin Coomber, c/o The Excelsior Hotel. He extracted a letter and photographed it. There would be time later for reading. The immediate priority was to move fast.

A cowboy film was showing on the TV screen and James Stewart as an army scout was giving drawling praise to the virtues of Apache warriors when there was a knock on the door. Samson snapped the suitcase shut and stood up as a hotel maid entered.

Her jaw slipped open as she saw Samson but before she could speak he held his briefcase triumphantly aloft and with a wide smile said, 'Good. I've found it! I was sure I'd left it here!'

The maid was still speechless as he walked past her but he noticed her eyes were fixed on the surgical gloves.

'Dermatitis,' he whispered. 'Very painful. Avoid it if you can.'

44

With that, he walked calmly out of the room. Once in the corridor he raced to the lift. It was with a feeling of relief that he passed through the hotel portals and made his way to the nearby underground station.

He didn't normally take work to his apartment but that evening, the film in his camera having been developed, he decided to study the prints. He had eaten well at an Indian restaurant in Soho and now sat in his favourite armchair with a glass of whisky next to him. On the radio an orchestra was playing a selection of melodies from *South Pacific*.

Before examining the photographed material he thought about the passport. Why hadn't the 'widow' noticed the absence of a passport among the effects handed to her after the death of a man in a road accident? Had shock and grief blocked out any estimate of what should have been found with the dead body? It might have.

It was difficult to assess Mary Coomber. According to Ruddick she was sweet, good-natured and somewhat naive. She had unremarkable looks and would pass anywhere as an unassuming suburban housewife. If she had noticed the absence of a passport among her husband's possessions she might have felt diffident about mentioning it to the police, but on balance it seemed more likely that the thought of a missing passport hadn't occurred to her.

He took another drink and then looked at the photocopy of the letter postmarked 'Bath'. It was signed 'Maureen'.

The letter was written in an immature sloping hand on one side of the paper. The margins were narrow and the capital letter 'I' was bowed rather than stiffly erect. In the past Samson had occasionally used the services of a graphologist and from him had picked up the rudiments of the study of handwriting. The narrow margins indicated a person who liked to fill every moment of life and the bowed 'I' could indicate flexibility or low self-esteem.

The upper zone of the writing was sparse and suggested limited imagination, the middle zone was well connected and showed the writer was well adjusted to her environment, and the florid lower zone indicated a strong sexual drive.

Having made a tentative analysis of the writer's character Samson read the letter.

My dearest darling,

It is now ten days since you left and I have heard from you only three times though you did promise to phone me every day. I can understand if you have been very busy and I know you are doing what you are doing for us both but I do need to hear from you darling. I hope you are successful in getting backing for something better than the video jokes. Incidentally I am still getting aggro from Mr Jenkins for the manure you dumped in his front garden. I have had to explain that you have gone away and I don't know your address. I love you very much and only want the best for you and to be with you always. Please ring or write. I miss you terribly.

With all my love,
Maureen

An address label at the top of the letter showed the sender to be Maureen Hislop of Pinetree Guest House, London Road, Bath. A telephone number, code 0225, appeared under the address.

For a few moments Samson considered the contents of the letter. It was obvious that Maureen Hislop was in love with Coomber and that she was probably the owner of a guest house. The allusion to video jokes was less easy to fathom but it seemed possible that these were unpleasant practical jokes on the lines of *Candid Camera*. Perhaps Coomber was commissioned by customers to make a video of a rival's, or an enemy's, discomfiture. For the manure-dumping joke Coomber was possibly filming from a van parked nearby. With luck he would catch the fury and frustration of the man whose front garden had suddenly become smothered in a pile of dung.

Samson put aside the letter and picked up photocopies of entries in the pink file. These showed that Coomber was proposing to move into a different sphere of video production. The budget figures showed that a million pounds was needed to back an hour-long film on the intricate relationship between fighting and love-making from myth to modern times. Written notes showed the project to be a hybrid of dubious educational merit and soft porn. Von Clausewitz's brutal maxim, 'Woman is the reward of the warrior', was written in capital letters and heavily underlined.

The project seemed genuine enough, if misguided, and not worth the expenditure of a million pounds. Samson put away the papers, switched off the radio and went to the bathroom for a relaxing hot bath. Tomorrow he'd begin the hard graft of finding out exactly why a second-hand Mercedes had been crashed shortly after its purchase.

It was raining on the following morning when Samson set out to make enquiries at Maurice Moxon Motors at Whetstone in north London. Within half an hour he was entering a large car showroom filled with gleaming new models. Outside, as if victims of class distinction, second-hand cars for sale stood in a row like rain-soaked outcasts.

Once inside the showroom Samson was approached by a young, well-dressed salesman who addressed him as 'Sir' and asked if he could be of any assistance.

Samson showed his visiting card and said, 'I'm making confidential enquiries on behalf of a relative about a car which was sold here two years ago. It was a white Mercedes, I don't know which marque, but it was six years old and belonged to someone who worked here. Can you help?'

The young man shook his head. 'I only started here five weeks ago but I'll ask the manager.' He gave Samson a quick look. 'While you're waiting you might like to have a look at this.' From a table he picked up a glossy brochure which advertised the latest model of a well-known German car. 'It's excellent value for money. If you'd like to see the real thing, there's one over there.' He pointed. 'They are prestige cars, sir.'

Samson was tempted to say, 'What makes you think I'm in need of a high-status product?' but he didn't want to alienate goodwill and he accepted the brochure. He glanced through it while the salesman went in search of the manager. Photographic illustrations showed a nubile young woman seated on the bonnet displaying lengths of shapely legs. Were there, Samson wondered, any men gullible enough to think that possession of a prestige car would collect the bonus gift of a woman like that? He reflected that possibly there were, and probably they were right. The merchantable value of sex knew no boundaries.

The manager was a short brisk man with a face like a pitted brick wall. 'Can I help you, sir?'

Samson went through his routine of making an enquiry on behalf of a relative.

'The police checked up on this a couple of years ago,' said the manager. 'So, what's new?'

'That is something I can't reveal,' said Samson, 'but it doesn't in any way put your man in difficulty. I know about the police enquiry. I have a lot of friends in the police force, incidentally. But the police enquiry was limited to the single fact that a sale was made. The relative who I represent wants to know if at any time anything was said about where the purchaser intended to go, where he intended taking the car.' He lowered his voice. 'To be frank, it's someone who was bereaved by the accident and can't get over it. Wants to know every least little thing about the deceased man's last hours and a psychiatrist has recommended that this wish be gratified. In my opinion, it's a load of rubbish, but it's what I'm paid to do. Can you help?'

A crack appeared in the brick wall and not for the first time Samson realised that mention of a psychiatrist was the key to many closed doors. Although by some they

48

were regarded as trick cyclists riding on the tightrope of some sucker's neurosis, by others they were looked on as sophisticated witch doctors who should be treated with respect, if not deference.

The manager was in the latter category. 'The car was sold by Chris,' he said.

'Thank you.'

Two minutes later a man in white overalls inscribed with the initials 'MMM' in red appeared.

Samson went through his routine again finishing with, 'Mr Coomber's relative is anxious to know about everything that was said.'

'I don't remember much, sir. The car was out on the forecourt. The customer came in and said he'd like to buy. It happened that half the sales staff were away with 'flu and most of the others were at lunch and I was standing in. I sold it within two minutes and he drove it away after Marjorie – she's the cashier – had arranged the insurance and done the paperwork. I don't remember nothing else.'

'He didn't say where he was going?'

The mechanic frowned. 'It was a long time ago . . . But . . . Half a minute . . . He said something about fancying a pub lunch. Yeah, that's it. He fancied a pub lunch and he asked me if there was a good pub near here.'

'What did you tell him?'

'I don't remember. There are a few pubs round here. The Black Bull and others. I think I told him the names.'

'But you don't know which one he went to?'

'No, sir.'

'Was there anything else he said you can remember?'

'No, sir. He seemed in a bit of a hurry.'

'How did he pay?'

'In cash, sir. In American dollars. Marjorie said it was all right and she'd get it changed into sterling. It was actually my car, you see, but I was selling it through the firm.'

'How did he strike you? Did he seem confident and relaxed or was he nervous?'

The mechanic's frown deepened. 'It's hard to say. He did seem a bit edgy perhaps. Like I say, he was in a hurry. Oh, yes. And there's something else I remember. He smoked a lot. He offered me a fag.'

'Did you accept it?'

'Oh no, sir. I'm a non-smoker,' replied the mechanic self-righteously.

Samson took out his wallet and extracted a five-pound note. 'I won't suggest you buy cigarettes,' he said, 'but have a drink on me tonight.'

After asking for directions to the Black Bull he climbed into his car and drove away. The time had come to undertake the routine of going from place to place, armed with a photograph, and asking a series of strangers whether they recognised the face in the photograph. This was often a tedious and frustrating business and it sometimes received the coldly dismissive reaction many people give to an unwanted door-to-door salesman. But, although he embarked on the wearisome routine with the reluctance of a cat entering water, once committed to the course of action he became as dedicated to the pursuit as any cat absorbed with chasing and cornering a mouse.

He drew a blank at the Black Bull but at the third local pub he visited his determination was rewarded.

5

Samson wasn't obsessive about observing drink–drive guide-
lines but today he stuck rigidly to a non-alcoholic brand of
beer. The landlord was serving behind the bar. As he paid
for the drink Samson said, 'I'm a private enquiry agent acting
in a missing-person case and I'd welcome your help. Do you
recognise this man?'

After peering at the photograph the landlord replied,
'I see hundreds of customers but the face is vaguely familiar.'

'He might have called in here for a drink and lunch just
over two years ago. He came in a white Mercedes which
would probably have been parked in your car park. But someone else was found in the Mercedes when it crashed. It looks
as though his car might have been thieved by someone.'

'Cars are left at owners' risk,' said the landlord defen-
sively.

'Yes, I know that. There's no question of liability on
your part. I'm simply trying to establish who was in the
car when it crashed.'

The pub was beginning to fill up with customers.

'Excuse me a minute,' said the landlord and he went
to serve a couple of tall men, one of whom was carrying
a golf club.

Samson sat on a bar stool and looked around. The pub
was typical of hundreds with its fake oak beams, burnished
horse brasses, reproduction wheelback chairs, durable red
carpet and, in a far corner, a dartboard.

The landlord, having served two lagers, returned. 'Sorry,

what were you saying? Something about a Merc being pinched from my car park?'

'That's right. Do you remember the incident?'

The landlord puckered his lips as though preparing to blow a trumpet. After holding the embouchure for a few moments he said, 'I can remember one incident and it was about two years ago. It could have been that fellow in your photo . . . Excuse me.'

More customers had drifted in and the only assistant, a heavily built barmaid, was having difficulty coping with a stream of orders. Samson realised that interruptions would be continuous. He placed a briefcase on the counter. A built-in microphone was connected to a tape-recorder inside the case. Later he would ask Georgia to transcribe the disjointed conversation with the landlord.

It was early evening when Georgia presented him with the transcript. 'I hope I've done it right,' she said. 'It wasn't easy. I had to cut out bits of talk the mike picked up between a couple of golf fanatics.'

Samson took the typescript. 'Thanks. And thanks for staying late.'

She smiled. 'My pleasure. I want to make the grade.'

'Tomorrow I've got another job for you. I want you to find out where the local press for the Welwyn and Hatfield area has its HQ. Visit and ask to see copies of their paper for the twenty-second of March onwards two years ago. You'll be looking for reports of a fatal road accident at a railway bridge. What I particularly want, if it's given, is the name and address of the witness who came across the accident and informed the police. This might appear as a news item or, at a later date, at the coroner's inquest. Okay?'

Georgia nodded. 'Fine.'

'The man who died, or is reputed to have died, in the crash is someone called Colin Coomber.'

'Right.'

She left the room and Samson began reading.

I've been thinking some more about it, that fellow in your photo. There was an incident about two years ago. The first I knew something was up was when one of my customers, he's a regular, over seventy, drives an old Jag XJ6 which is his pride and joy, keeps it in mint condition, well, he staggered in looking for all the world as if he was going to collapse with a heart attack. Turns out his precious Jag has been hijacked . . . As I remember it, what had happened was that your chap, the one in the photo, had just left this house to go to his car, and must have seen it being thieved because my customer had just driven in and was about to get out of his car, had opened the door, when he was unceremoniously bundled out by your chap . . . He said, and I can recall the words exactly because my customer couldn't get over the shock and kept repeating them. Your chap said, 'Some bastard's nicked my car, I'm borrowing yours.' . . . It all comes back to me now. Funny thing, memory. Where had I got to? Oh yes, my customer was sent sprawling and when he got up he saw his Jag being driven away at high speed. Of course we phoned the police . . . It was a foggy day and bloody dangerous for a car chase. Never knew what happened. But, believe it or not, the Jag turned up again. It was after pub closing hours in the afternoon and no one saw it being parked but there it was, parked in our park here. Returned. Not damaged either. Still in mint condition. But whether your chap's car was a white Merc, I don't know. All I know is that someone borrowed and then returned the Jag. I assume he never caught whoever had pinched his car. Funny business . . . No, the police didn't come up with anything. I think they wrote it off as a bit of joy-riding and my customer was so pleased to have his car back he didn't want to push things. It was all over and done within a couple of hours at most.

Samson put down the typescript. Georgia had done a good job and included all essentials. Evidence of an opportunist disappearing act was mounting. If Coomber had left his suitcase and credit cards in the crashed Mercedes, and put his ring on the finger of the dead thief, he had also presumably removed all evidence of the other man's identity. The police hadn't followed up enquiries because it didn't appear that a crime had been committed. A fatal accident had occurred and although suicide might have been suspected nobody had raised this issue. The accident, it was assumed, had been caused by driving too fast in treacherous weather conditions.

The following day Georgia went to the offices of the *Welwyn Weekly Press* and returned with the information Samson needed. The man who had reported the accident was a Mr Scales who lived at an address at Welham Green in Hertfordshire. He had been walking along a deserted country lane with his dog. The fog had been patchy but quite thick in parts. When he came near to the railway bridge which spanned the road he had seen a white shape crushed against the bridge. He had run to the nearest house and telephoned the police.

At the inquest a verdict of accidental death was recorded. Blood samples had been taken but no traces of alcohol were found. However, the coroner took the opportunity of open court to comment that if the deceased had been wearing his safety belt, as required by law, he might still be alive.

A faintly sardonic smile momentarily lightened Samson's well-worn face as he reflected that people who make fast getaways in stolen cars don't normally consider legal requirements.

Having skimmed through photostats of newspaper cuttings he looked up at Georgia, who was standing near his desk. 'Nothing much here,' he said.

'No, but we've got a name.'

'You've read up the file – Mr Ruddick's file – have you?'

'Of course. I'm interested, really interested, in all our cases, even the routine ones.'

'Have you got any views?'

The question wasn't asked because Samson was short of ideas; it was another test of Georgia's capabilities. She reacted with a look of intense concentration which somehow aged her so that Samson had a preview of how she might appear in ten or fifteen years' time.

'If I was you – sorry, grammar again – if I *were* you I'd go to that address in Bath and suss things out.'

Samson nodded approvingly. 'Good. That's my next step after seeing Mr Scales.'

'Do you want me to check whether he's on the phone and make an appointment for you?'

'No. There are times when surprise is more effective. People forewarned of a visit by a private detective don't experience the same warm anticipation they'd give to a call by a football pools rep with news of a giant win. They feel defensive. They'll say things like, "I don't want to be involved." We live in a world where non-involvement is the gut reaction to anything concerning the death of a stranger.'

'I see . . . Is there anything else you want me to do on the case, Mr Samson?'

'Not at the moment.'

'Am I doing all right?'

'You're doing very well, Georgia.'

'This is my big chance. I don't want to make a cock of it.'

'What you can do is make me a coffee.'

'Will do.'

She tripped out of the room, legs twinkling, head held high.

Samson's eyes, less sleepy than usual, followed her progress with an avuncular look. He had rescued her from the blight of a life which depended on hooking punters from the street. He was not a Gladstone, or a moral crusader, but he liked quietly to help those who through no fault of their own were channelled in the loser's lane. He had once nearly been a loser himself.

* * *

Various light industries had mushroomed round the village of Welham Green, which was set in one of the flatter parts of the Home Counties. Rows of council houses made it impossible for the village to qualify as stockbroker belt – it was more of a DIY girth – and it was at a council house, red-bricked and in a terrace of identically anonymous houses, that Samson called.

A dog barked when he rang the doorbell. Moments later a man in pullover, baggy trousers and carpet slippers appeared holding a Dalmatian dog by its collar. The man had a peaky face and deep lines bracketed his nose and mouth; he had the joyless look of someone who has forgotten how to smile.

'Mr Scales?' enquired Samson.

'Yes.'

'I've come on behalf of a bereaved relative of someone who died in a tragic accident. I'd be grateful if you'd spare me five minutes of your time.'

'Who are you?'

'Here is my card. You can keep it,' said Samson magnanimously handing over a card, 'but I'm not investigating or detecting anything sinister. I'm merely here on doctor's orders.'

'Doctor's orders?'

'The person I represent is suffering deep depression. She wants to know everything possible about someone who died and a psychiatrist recommended that her wish be met.'

There was no change of expression on Scales's bleakly impassive face but his voice was a shade warmer as he asked, 'How can I help?'

'If you could just spare me five minutes . . . I know my client would wish me to remunerate you for any inconvenience caused.'

'Pay me, you mean?'

'Say ten or fifteen pounds. It will literally only be five minutes. I simply want you to tell me what happened on the twenty-second of March two years ago.'

56

Scales looked nonplussed. 'I haven't a clue.'

'You found a wrecked car. The driver was dead.'

'Oh, that. I told the police everything I could at the time.'

'I know you did. And you behaved in a very public-spirited way, or so they informed me. But that isn't the point. I have a client with a nervous illness who wants me to hear your version all over again.'

Scales hesitated. 'It's draughty standing here,' he said at length. 'You'd better come in.'

He led the way to a small kitchen at the back of the house. His dog and Samson followed.

'You must take me as you find me,' said Scales. 'I live alone with Simon here. Would you like to sit down?'

He indicated a chair beside the kitchen table from which the remains of a meal hadn't been cleared. Samson noticed a large bone, with fragments of meat clinging to it, lying in the middle of the room. The place smelled of stale cooking.

Scales took a small chair which stood in a corner and brought it to the table to sit opposite Samson. Without preamble he launched into a story which had been told many times. It was a straightforward account of being the first on the scene of an accident.

'And you hadn't heard the car crash?' Samson asked.

'I don't remember any particular noise. I know there was a train passing about that time. I heard its hooter.'

'The house where you called the police from – did the people there hear anything?'

'Not that I know of.'

'I imagine the man looked in a bad way.'

Scales sat upright in his chair. 'In a bad way!' he exclaimed, 'I've only once seen anything like it in my life and that was when I was in the army and my pal had his face blown half-off by a grenade. Unrecognisable as a human being he was.'

'And there was no road traffic? No other cars?'

57

'Not a thing.'

'And you don't know of anyone who might have seen another car around the time of the accident?'

The dog, which had been watching Samson, decided to settle on the floor and to gnaw at its bone.

'There's a good boy,' said Scales fondly, and then, turning to Samson, 'Another car, did you say?'

'Yes.'

'Funny you should ask that. We dog-walkers are a fraternity, if you take my meaning. We might not see each other for weeks and then we do for two or three days on the trot. And Simon there is a good dog, he gets on well with other dogs. Maybe I'll let him have a little run around with another dog while I have a word or two with its master. Well, about a fortnight after the accident I met this chap with a springer spaniel, Henry by name. The dog that is, not its master, who is a Mr Bunting, a retired gentleman like me. He said to me, "I see you are famous. You've got your name in the papers." He was joking, of course. I'm not really famous. But that's by the way. We got to talking and I remarked how strange it was that there wasn't any other car around and he reminded me that there had been drainage works at the end of the lane which had temporarily closed that end. A diversion had been signposted. I don't run a car and that sort of thing doesn't affect me. Well, coming from the other end of the lane, as that poor fellow must have done, he must have missed the diversion sign, it being a foggy day, and driven straight on past it and . . . '

'Just a moment,' Samson interrupted. 'Do you mean that if he had passed under the bridge he would eventually have found the lane blocked off?'

'That's right.'

'And so he would have been obliged to turn round and retrace his route?'

'That's it exactly. But what I'm coming to is this. Mr Bunting was at the far end of the lane that day and someone who was driving away from the direction of the bridge passed him, and passed him so close he was nearly killed. The man was driving like a maniac.'

'Did Mr Bunting describe the car to you?'

'It was a black car.'

'An XJ6?'

Scales gave a quavery laugh. 'It's no use asking me, is it? I don't know a thing about cars. I've never owned one and never want to.'

'But might Mr Bunting know?'

'He might.'

The dog left its bone and crossed the kitchen to lap at water from a bowl near the sink.

'Have you got a dog?' Scales asked.

'No.'

'Man's best friend. No doubt about it. Better than a woman any day. Never answers back. Always grateful for what you give them. A companion through thick and thin. I'll tell you something. I wouldn't swap Simon for Joan Collins or the Duchess of York or anyone you care to name.'

'Both ladies would be deeply upset if they knew you'd said that,' said Samson, 'but rest assured, I won't tell either of them. By the way, where does Mr Bunting live?'

'In Bell Bar. That's a locality not far from here. I sometimes walk there with Simon.'

'Do you know his exact address?'

'It's in Bell Lane. I don't know its number but it's called Bellman's Cottage, which is daft because it isn't a cottage and there's never been a bellman, whatever that might be.'

Samson rose to his feet. 'You've been very helpful, Mr Scales.' He produced three five-pound notes. 'I'd like you to take this for your trouble. Treat Simon to something really tasty and have a drink on me yourself.'

Bellman's Cottage was a detached mock-Tudor house set back from the road. A burglar alarm was prominently displayed on its façade and, according to a sticker near the front door, the owner was a member of Neighbourhood Watch.

The door was opened by a middle-aged woman who held a cigarette in her hand. Samson, self-trained to observe the smallest detail, noted that it was a Cartier, one of the more expensive brands. He said, 'I've just been talking to a Mr Scales of Welham Green. He's referred me to Mr Bunting.'

The woman turned her head. 'Jim,' she called out in a deep hoarse voice, 'it's for you.'

A short, square-jawed man with a weather-beaten face appeared. 'Yes? What is it?'

Samson produced his card. 'I'm making enquiries on behalf of someone whose close relative was killed in a car crash two years ago. Mr Scales thought you might be able to help.'

'Scales? Who's he?'

Samson was taken aback but didn't show it. With aplomb which would have been an object lesson to Georgia he said, 'He's Simon's master. I believe Simon is quite friendly with your Henry.'

'Oh, I know who you mean. Of course I do. Nothing the matter with Simon, I hope.'

'Nothing at all. He had a big bone and plenty of water.'

'Soppy dogs, Dalmatians. Walt Disney knew that. If you want a real dog get a springer spaniel.'

'I'll remember that advice. But I came here to ask you about something which happened a couple of years ago.'

Bunting examined Samson's card. 'You're an investigator?'

'I am.'

'You're not from Crufts?'

'No, I'm not from Crufts. Someone was killed in a road accident. He crashed into a bridge on a foggy day. I've been retained by a relative to make some enquiries.'

'Ah, yes. Now I've got it. Memory going. Scales was the

fellow who found the *corpus delicti*, wasn't he? Remember it now. Pulled his leg a bit. Don't think he liked it.'

'Might I ask you a question or two?'

'I don't know how I could help, but you'd better come in.'

Samson was taken to a room filled with antique furniture, many pieces of which were garishly adorned with a mixture of cheap souvenirs from foreign parts. Some dolls in Spanish dress and a Hawaiian dancer doll lined the top of an eighteenth-century bureau and a spinet was almost invisible beneath draped Spanish shawls held down by two large china dogs which looked as though they had been won on a fairground. Pictures of boats lined the walls and beneath one large oil painting of a yacht in full sail was a ledge filled with silver cups and trophies.

'Would you like a cup of tea?' the woman asked in her throaty voice.

'I'd love one. No sugar, please.'

While she was out of the room Samson asked the vital questions. Had Bunting noticed the make of car which had passed close to him on the fatal day, and could he identify the driver from a photograph?

'It was an old Jag,' said Bunting, 'and I'd know the bugger who was driving it if I saw him again. The sod nearly killed me.'

'He was driving like a maniac?'

'You've got it in one.'

Samson produced a photograph of Colin Coomber. 'Do you recognise this man?'

Bunting studied the photo. 'It could be him. In fact, I'm virtually certain it is. Is he to be prosecuted for dangerous driving?'

'Not that I'm aware of.'

'That's good. I don't want to be involved.'

'Nobody ever does,' said Samson putting the photograph away.

'Is that all you want to know?'

'That's all.'

'Good. Won't ask what all this is about. Don't really want to know. Don't believe in sticking my nose into other people's business.'

Mrs Bunting entered pushing a tea trolley. For Samson the professional enquiry was over; now, to earn his cup of tea, he would have to engage in the social exercise of conversation. This wasn't as boring as he anticipated. It transpired that Bunting was a keen yachtsman and had a ketch berthed on the River Hamble. He went sailing whenever he could. He had also once commanded a minesweeper and, as Samson had many years before been a rating in the Royal Navy, they were able to exchange reminiscences.

He left Bellman's Cottage well satisfied with the afternoon's work. There was no doubt that Coomber had taken the opportunity of another man's death to fake his own. The alleged amnesia was almost certainly also faked. A trip to Bath should put the seal on that line of enquiry.

6

In Samson's opinion motor cars were functional utilities serving purpose, not pleasure. Talk about torque bored him and he was more interested in hotel bars than anti-roll bars. Nevertheless, he had a fair mechanical knowledge of cars and was an expert driver. He covered the 120-mile run to Bath from London's West End in eighty minutes and was lucky not to be booked for speeding by police patrols.

Pinetree Guest House was set well back from a main road from which it was separated by a low brick wall and an immaculately kept grass lawn. Samson was amused to see a small notice beside the path leading to the front door which read, 'Please do not walk on the grass'.

He rang the bell and the door was opened by a woman who looked as though she was in her early forties. She was small, pretty and blonde, and she possessed an indefinable air of womanly comfort. She gave Samson a warm smile.

'Do you have a room for the night?' he asked.

'As a matter of fact I do. There is one room.'

'One room is fine. Half a room wouldn't be quite enough.'

Her smile widened and she gave a laugh which vibrated her bosom. 'Please come in,' she said.

Before signing the register he read a notice and tariff pinned to a wall above a bowl of flowers. 'You are Mrs Hislop, a co-proprietor,' he asked.

'That's me, but everyone calls me Maureen.' She gave a little giggle. 'I think it's nice to use first names. Freddie, he's my husband, is different. He likes to be called Mr Hislop.

Not that he minds me being called Maureen,' she went on hurriedly. 'In fact, he quite encourages the familiarity.'

Samson took out a pen and signed the register 'John Dan'. According to the Book of Judges the biblical Samson came from the tribe of Dan, and it appealed to his whimsical humour to use the name when he wanted to be incognito.

Maureen Hislop peered at the register. 'Welcome to Pinetree, Mr Dan. I'll show you to your room.'

It was a typical British guest-house room with a wash-basin in one corner, plain dressing table and old-fashioned wardrobe. The wallpaper was pink and green Regency pattern which clashed with a large framed reproduction of a painting depicting a waving yellow cornfield under a blazing blue sky.

'Will the room suit, Mr Dan?'

'It'll suit me well.'

'If there's anything you need, we're at your service.'

She left the room. After depositing his overnight bag and washing his hands Samson decided to take a stroll round the city centre.

It was evening and most of the stores had closed but he wasn't concerned with shopping; he wanted to find a good place to dine. It was as he paused before an elegant Georgian house which had been converted into a restaurant that he knew he had arrived at his destination. It was called Popjoy's Restaurant and a plaque stated that the house had once been the residence of Beau Nash and his mistress, Juliana Popjoy. Beau Nash had died there in February 1761. A menu posted near the entrance listed an appealing choice of dishes.

Shandy wouldn't have approved but he started with lamb's sweetbreads *en brioche* and followed this with breast of guinea fowl stuffed with crab. For dessert he enjoyed crème caramel with coconut purée. The meal was accompanied by a bottle of chablis from Meursault. Samson was used to dining alone, and generally preferred it, but tonight for some inexplicable reason he wondered for a few idle moments what it would have been like to have had Maureen Hislop as his companion.

On returning to the guest house he took advantage of a notice which stated that if refreshment was needed – tea, coffee or liquor – the guest should press a bell-push. Samson pressed. After a few moments Maureen Hislop appeared.

'Is it too late to ask for a whisky?' he enquired.

'Not at all, Mr Dan. Never too late for anything.' She gave her ready smile and he understood why he had briefly thought of her in the restaurant. She had an attractively outgoing warmth, an air of emotional generosity, which was positive and strong enough even to reach someone as toughly insular as he. 'I'll ask my husband to bring it up to your room,' she said. 'We have Bell's, Teachers or Johnny Walker Black Label.'

'I'll have Black Label please. A large one.'

As he climbed a narrow staircase he wondered whether his curiosity about human behaviour would ever wither and die. Creeping cynicism was one enemy of curiosity. It would be easy to be dismissively cynical about the drives, motivations and impulses of fellow human beings but if cynicism ever took a firm hold he felt his natural curiosity would be strangled. Perhaps the softest target for creeping cynicism was marriage. Cynicism was, after all, the comfort of the disillusioned. Maureen Hislop was yet another married woman having a love affair while playing the role of dutiful wife at home.

Once inside his room he kicked off his shoes and sat on the side of the bed waiting for Hislop to bring whisky. Did the man know of his wife's affair? And did she know that the other man was trying to get financial backing from *his* wife? Did she even know of the existence of a wife?

A faint knock on the door and Hislop entered carrying a tray on which was a glass of whisky, a small jug of water and a bottle of soda water.

'Maureen forgot to ask if you wanted anything with your drink,' he said. 'Soda water or clear water?'

'I'll have it neat, thanks,' replied Samson taking the glass. 'Are you a whisky-drinker?'

Hislop was a small wiry man with wispy grey hair. Beady eyes were close set in a narrow pointed face. Samson estimated that he was about twenty years older than his wife.

'Oh yes, I like a tot in the evening, Mr Dan. It's nice to have a little luxury at the end of the day.'

'And your day is pretty busy, I imagine. Hard work running a guest house.'

Hislop shook his head. 'Not so hard really. Not for me. Maureen does it mostly. I do the paperwork. The accounting side. I was in accountancy, you see. In a small way, that is. Clerical mainly. Er, what is your line, might I enquire?'

When wanting to establish a cover Samson generally used his expertise in clocks and timepieces. 'My interests are horological,' he said. 'Part of the year I travel round looking for antique or unusual clocks to purchase, whether they are in good working order or not.'

'Horological?' Hislop gave a little snicker. 'That's a good word . . . Will you be staying with us long?'

'Probably only tonight. I might go to Bristol tomorrow. Do you know Bristol?'

'I don't, but Maureen does. She comes from there. Bristol born and bred.' A glitter came to the twin brown beads of Hislop's eyes. 'Good stuff comes out of Bristol, Mr Dan. I'm a lucky man.'

'And I expect she'd say the same of you,' said Samson.

This time Hislop didn't snicker, he laughed outright. It was a peculiarly rasping sound. 'Lucky to have me!' he exclaimed. 'You must be joking. I'm old enough to be her dad. But I am fit, very physically fit, and I'm a very tolerant man. Those are my advantages. Fitness and tolerance.'

Samson was aware that some sort of message was being transmitted. Was Hislop tolerant of his wife's affair, or affairs?

'Might I ask, Mr Dan, do you travel much?'

'Quite a lot.'

'Ah. A lonely life I should think.'

'Very lonely sometimes.'

'Yes, it must be. We often get single men here as guests. Company reps mainly. We try to make them feel at home. Maureen is very good at that. We haven't got any kids. I think it's her mothering instincts. To be kind to single, lonely men, I mean. And not just young men either. Lonely men.'

An eagerness had entered Hislop's demeanour and Samson, who had been toying with his whisky, took a sip. 'It's a good thing to be kind to lonely men,' he said, 'and good of you to be understanding. Tolerant.'

'Some men wouldn't be, but I am. Mind you, it mustn't go too far, if you understand me.'

Samson feigned incomprehension. 'Too far?'

'Put it like this. Ships that pass in the night is one thing. Putting down anchor is something quite different. I wouldn't tolerate that.'

'There must be some,' said Samson thoughtfully, 'who could get the wrong impression and try to put down anchor when they find a woman who is kind to them.'

'Exactly right, Mr Dan. There was one such just recently. Tried to run a business from here, if you please. He had to go.'

'Stupid of him,' Samson commented.

'It was.'

'What sort of business did this man run?' asked Samson.

'Videos. He did a few weddings and suchlike functions, and then he had the idea of making embarrassing videos for a price. Having innocent men confronted by a prostitute in a public place, for instance, making out that the man was a punter who hadn't paid his dues. Or planting a bug in a car so that when the driver started the engine a woman's voice screamed, "Rape!" His customers were people who wanted to get their own back on somebody or play a practical joke.'

67

'I wouldn't have thought that sort of thing went down well with someone kind-hearted like your wife.'

'I don't think it did, Mr Dan. She's had to put up with hassle. And I had to be very firm indeed. I gave him his marching orders. And he had the cheek to say he wasn't being chucked out; he was going anyway as something better had turned up.'

'That's interesting,' said Samson. 'I once knew of someone who made videos of kissograms being delivered, boozy office parties, that sort of thing. What was the name of this fellow you were telling me about?'

'His name?'

'Yes.'

'He booked in as Vernon Brown.'

'Doesn't ring a bell,' said Samson, 'where did this Vernon Brown come from?'

'That's another story. He was born in Bristol like Maureen. They never knew each other there but it turned out they had one or two mutual acquaintances. A bit of a coincidence, that. Of course, it made him a winner with Maureen. A winner. But, as I say, I'm a tolerant man.'

Samson took another drink of whisky and then said, 'It seems to me he dropped anchor, as you put it.'

A shifty expression crossed Hislop's features. 'I see what you're getting at. One minute I say I won't have guests dropping anchor and the next I'm telling you about one who did. Well, there were special circumstances. A bit unusual you might think but we're all adults, aren't we. But my toleration was stretched too far when he started this business which he called "Video Vengeances". It attracted unwelcome publicity. Wedding photos is one thing but having muck dumped on other people's front lawns is something else. That's a terrible thing to do. He had to go.'

'It doesn't sound like the man I knew,' said Samson, 'he came from Cheshire and apart from the kissogram videos he had a market stall, selling clothes and fabrics. What was your man doing before he arrived on your doorstep?'

'That, Mr Dan, was a bit of a mystery. He arrived, well dressed, with enough money to get by on, but couldn't seem to remember where his home was. He could remember bits of his childhood in Bristol and early life but had a memory blockage after that. When I suggested the police might be able to help he clammed up. Said he didn't like or trust the police. Maureen backed him up on that. But that's another story. She's got reasons. I don't know what reasons he had.'

A silence fell. It was broken by Hislop.

'I'd better be going. If you want anything in the night I shall probably be sound asleep but Maureen is a very light sleeper. She's in the room directly above yours and if there's anything you need, anything at all, I feel sure she would oblige. It won't disturb me. We sleep in separate rooms.'

'Thank you,' said Samson, 'but I don't expect I shall need anything.'

'Well, if you do, she's in the room above. She won't mind being disturbed. She enjoys company. Loves to talk. She's very understanding.' Hislop turned. 'I'll bid you good night.'

For a while Samson thought about the case. He was no nearer discovering whether the amnesia was genuine but the trip to Bath hadn't been a waste of professional time. He had learned that Coomber had used the alias of Vernon Brown and that Maureen Hislop, if he interpreted her husband's coded messages correctly, gave intimate meaning to the phrase 'bed and breakfast'.

It wasn't unknown for old men to be tolerant of their younger wives' caprices, and even to act as pander, but how had these two come to marry? Hislop appeared to have little going in his favour whereas his wife had a charming smile, vitality and earth-mother appeal. What had she seen in him? The thought crossed Samson's mind that they could have worked in the same office and she had stolen money or participated in some sort of fraud. Hislop had discovered this and used it to blackmail her into marriage in return for him concealing the fraud. He might have agreed that she could always have other bed partners but if she stretched his toleration too far he would threaten to disclose what he knew.

But these were conjectures and had little or no bearing on the case in hand. He finished his whisky, read a few pages of a paperback book and was about to get ready to retire for the night when there was a knock on the door.

'Come in.'

Maureen Hislop entered. She was wearing a peach-coloured housecoat and fur-trimmed mules on her feet.

'I hope I'm not disturbing you, Mr Dan, but Freddie completely forgot to ask what you'd like for breakfast. I can do you a full English breakfast or just coffee and rolls, whatever you'd like.'

'A full English breakfast,' said Samson after a moment's thought.

'Breakfast is between seven-thirty and nine.'

'I'll be down at eight.'

She smiled. 'Good. I like a man who's positive about what he wants and when . . . Is there anything else you'd like tonight?'

Her hand played with the belt of her housecoat and Samson wondered if she was about to loosen it.

He returned her smile. 'Thanks, but there's nothing else I need except a good night's sleep.'

'I hope you'll find the bed comfortable. I think you will. When convenient I make it my job to sleep in every bed in the house just to check that each one is really comfortable. A nice comfortable bed is so important, I think. After all, they say that on average we spend a third of our lives in bed.'

She spoke the word 'bed' with a sort of respectful soft-ness in the way a devoutly religious person might say 'holy communion' and perhaps, Samson later reflected, for her bed was a form of holy communion. But he simply said, 'I'm sure it'll be comfortable. Thank you for your consideration, Mrs Hislop. Good night and sleep well yourself.'

'Good night, Mr Dan.'

She sounded disappointed.

Moments later Samson could hear her moving in the room above and then there was silence. He switched out the light and thought about the coincidence which had brought Coomber/Brown to Bath and to Pinetree Guest House in particular. It was possibly no coincidence at all. Coomber and Maureen Hislop may have known each other as children in Bristol and not merely had 'mutual acquaintances' – that could have been just a line they fed to Hislop – and they could have kept in touch over the years. But whether or not a blow to the head in a Yorkshire pub had restored his memory of the address was an open question.

The following morning he entered the dining room promptly at eight. Maureen Hislop showed him to a small corner table. 'I hope you slept well, Mr Dan.'

'I did, and that's unusual. I'm not a good sleeper, but the bed was very comfortable.'

'Told you it was, didn't I?'

She didn't wait for a reply.

There were six other guests in the room; four were visitors from abroad and the other two were company representatives. Samson was the last to leave. After packing his overnight bag he went to the reception hall and pressed the bell-push. Maureen Hislop appeared from a back room.

'I'd like my bill, please.'

'Right. I'll get Freddie. He manages that side of things. Gives him an interest besides mending fuses, his weight-lifting and that blessed lawn.'

'The lawn?'

She glanced round to make sure she couldn't be overheard. 'Between you and me, Mr Dan, he has some strange ways. He puts up with some things other husbands wouldn't tolerate but let someone walk on that precious lawn and he gets really mad.'

'No wonder he didn't like that fellow who stayed here and arranged for muck to be spread on somebody's lawn.'

71

Her face seemed to freeze and her body stiffened.

'Did he tell you about that?'

'Last night when he brought up my drink.'

She clucked her tongue. 'One day,' she began but didn't finish the sentence. 'I'll go and fetch him,' she said.

'I believe he has accountancy experience,' said Samson quickly before she could turn away.

'You might call it that. He was a bank cashier.'

'And you worked in the same bank?'

She looked away. 'Only for a short while. I'll get Freddie.' She hurried towards the back room.

Hislop appeared almost at once.

'I hope you enjoyed your stay, Mr Dan.'

'Very pleasant, thanks.'

After perusing the bill Samson took out his wallet and peeled off some banknotes. He had once, when registered at a hotel as 'John Dan', offered a credit card in payment only to realise as he passed it over that the card was signed 'John Samson'. It was a mistake he was determined never to repeat.

As he was pocketing the receipt he said, 'By the way, do you know who this is?' He produced the photograph of Colin Coomber.

Hislop took one look and said, 'Of course I do. That's the man I was telling you about. Vernon Brown. Where did you get that?'

'I found it in my room. Under the bed. Near the bed-head. I'd dropped some small change and a coin rolled under the bed. I found it while I was groping around.'

Hislop's pointed features became even more pointed as though they'd been honed on a gigantic pencil-sharpener. 'Can't think how a picture of that sod got there,' he said.

'I've no idea either,' said Samson, 'but I'm sure you won't want it as a keepsake. I'll get rid of it for you.' He slipped the photo into his overnight bag. 'Good day, Mr Hislop.'

'Just a moment, sir, if you please. We have a guest

book for comments by guests. Would you care to write something about your stay here?'

'Certainly.'

Hislop handed him the book and Samson read some of the comments before writing his own. These were: 'Food excellent and hospitality even better!', 'Fantastic – every whim catered for', 'Good on you, Freddie, you're a real sport'.

Samson took out his pen and wrote, 'The consideration shown by Mr and Mrs Hislop matches the perfection of the lawn which fronts their house.'

'Will that do?' he asked.

'Absolutely, Mr Dan. I can see you are a real gentleman.'

Like many private investigators Samson had contacts in the police force. He contributed regularly to funds for police dependants and whenever possible gave assistance to police enquiries. On one occasion he had trapped and effected a citizen's arrest on an arsonist, and on another he had rescued an off-duty woman police constable who was being molested in a subway by three youths. For such co-operation and assistance he was sometimes able to ask for information on the police computer about a named person. His principal contact was on the staff at New Scotland Yard.

Once back in London he telephoned his contact. Because of adverse publicity about the revelation of information from confidential police sources to independent detective agencies, Samson simply asked the contact, Bernard, to meet him for a drink. On any tape of the conversation it would appear that the call was purely for social purposes.

They met at a pub, the Two Chairmen, near Queen Anne's Gate. Bernard had never heard of Vernon Brown but promised to find out whether he had a criminal record. He was grateful for Samson's unsolicited gift of a bottle of champagne with which to wet the head of his new-born child.

On the following day Samson received a call from a

public phone-booth. The caller didn't identify himself but simply said, 'Your man is a car thief. Three convictions. Psychiatrist at the third court hearing said Brown had an uncontrollable impulse to steal cars. The court couldn't have been very impressed with this defence and Brown got six months in the nick.'

Samson thanked his caller. Although the information was incidental to his main enquiry he was building up a comprehensive picture of the missing years in Colin Coomber's life. Coomber had unwittingly taken on the identity of a dead and unmourned car thief.

7

On his way to meet Bernard, Samson had seen an estate agent's board advertising the letting of a flat in the vicinity of Queen Anne's Gate. Following the call from Bernard about Vernon Brown's criminal record he told Shandy he was considering asking for an appointment to view the flat. 'What you need,' she said, 'is a good woman. That would settle you.'

'The fact that I'm thinking of moving to a new apartment doesn't mean I'm unsettled or need a good woman. I'd sooner be single than one half of a couple and that's the end of it.'

'Some people say the world is made for couples,' she went on, blithely ignoring his hint that discussion on the matter was ended. 'Two by two into the ark, and all that.'

'All right then, and since you won't drop the subject, we'll talk about couples. Would you say that Ruddick and Mary Coomber are a couple, or is the couple Colin Coomber and Mary?'

She thought for a moment. 'Maybe the world is really made for triangles,' she said, 'but I hope not.'

'Speaking of which, I must give our client a call.'

Samson left her and went to his room. He picked up a handset and keyed a number.

'Mr Ruddick? Samson here. Is it convenient to speak?'

'Yes. Go ahead.'

'This is an interim report. The man who died in the car crash was a convicted thief, Vernon Brown. It looks as though Mr Coomber took on his identity and for a while lived under that name in bed and breakfast accommodation in Bath.'

Samson heard an intake of breath. And then, 'You're sure about this?'

'I'm certain.'

'So the amnesia story is complete rubbish?'

'It seems so.'

'Can you actually prove he never suffered amnesia?'

'Not yet.'

'I see. Well, I hope you will bear in mind the terms of our agreement. The deal was that you would obtain proof that he never had amnesia and returned to Mary simply to improve his finances. Those were the conditions to be fulfilled in return for your fee which, I have to say, I still consider exorbitant.'

'You don't need to remind me of the terms of our agreement,' replied Samson sharply. 'This is, as I said, an interim report. And I should like to make a slight correction to what you've just said. I undertook to obtain *evidence*, not *proof*, that Mr Coomber never suffered amnesia.'

'I stand corrected on that minor detail. I should like to come and see you. Could we make it some time tomorrow?'

Samson reached for his desk diary. 'Would eleven a.m. suit you?'

'I'd prefer a late appointment. I have a business to manage.'

'Six in the evening?'

'That would suit me better. I'll see you then.'

Samson tried to adopt an attitude of neutrality when dealing with his clients and, on an emotional level, to remain uninvolved with their problems. However, this stance wasn't always easy to maintain. Occasionally it was impossible not to feel deep sympathy for some and harsh feelings towards others. Ruddick was swiftly moving into the latter category.

His opinion of Ruddick wasn't improved when his client

appeared promptly at six the following day accompanied by a woman Samson recognised as Mary Coomber.

'You've brought an associate with you, Mr Ruddick?' he asked smoothly.

'Not an associate, no. This is the lady I hope to marry one day. I've brought Mrs Coomber along so that she can hear what you told me yesterday.'

Mary Coomber, who was wearing a high-necked lilac blouse under a two-piece dove-grey suit, gave a nervous smile as a flush came to her cheeks. Above dark-blue eyes her eyebrows contracted slightly as though she was trying to place Samson as someone she'd seen somewhere before.

He returned her smile and hoped she wouldn't connect him with the Oslo Court restaurant. So far as he was aware, she hadn't noticed him there. Suppressing annoyance at Ruddick for the unwarranted introduction of a third party to the conference he said, 'Please take a seat, Mrs Coomber,' and he gave an airy gesture of his hand towards a green leather-backed chair.

She gave Ruddick a quick look as if to check that it was in order for her to sit down and then moved quickly to the chair Samson had indicated. Something in her bearing made him wonder if she was accustomed to a role of obedience. Once seated she crossed her legs demurely and tugged her skirt down. Ruddick was more leisurely in accommodating his lean frame to another chair.

'Now tell Mary just what you told me,' he said. 'Let her hear it straight from the horse's mouth.' He gave a weakly ingratiating smile.

'Ah, yes. The horse's mouth. Have you any idea how the saying originated?'

Ruddick was disconcerted. 'Er, from examining a horse's mouth to ascertain its true age, I'd guess. One gets truth from the horse's mouth.'

Samson nodded. 'Quite. But I have to tell you that you can take a horse to the water but you can't make him drink.'

Ruddick jerked upright in his chair. 'Does that mean you aren't prepared to speak about what you've discovered?'

'Not at all,' said Samson affably. 'I'm not a horse and so far I'm prepared to oblige you.' He swivelled in his chair to face Mary Coomber. 'I hope I won't be flogging a dead horse by continuing with horsey analogies,' he said, 'but my investigation leads me to think your husband is a dark horse.'

Out of the corner of his eye he was aware of Ruddick shifting angrily in his chair. It was, he decided, time to stop riling a client whom he disliked. He continued to address Mary Coomber and was surprised to see a mischievous twinkle in her eyes. Her face had a naturally gentle expression but, in spite of appearances, and the impression given by Ruddick at previous meetings, Samson sensed from the twinkle that she couldn't be written off as a pliant yes-woman.

'I'll try to be brief,' he said. 'As of course you know, your husband wasn't killed in a car accident. The man who died was one Vernon Brown, who was a known car thief. Since nobody was present at the accident Mr Coomber was able to assume the dead man's identity. A period elapsed about which I know nothing but he surfaced at a guest house in Bath under the name of Vernon Brown. He lived there for a while and made videos of weddings and other functions as a commercial enterprise. He also made videos of embarrassing situations for the benefit of malicious viewers. From Bath he came to London, his memory restored – if it had ever been missing – and made contact with you.'

'He told me he was working in a bar in Yorkshire when a fight broke out,' she said. 'Someone hit him over the head with a bottle.' She spoke in a soft voice and Samson thought he detected the trace of a north-country accent. 'He told me that the blow brought back his memory.'

'That may have happened. I can't prove or disprove it. But what I can prove is that he resided in Bath for some time under an assumed name.'

Ruddick, who had been fidgeting, spoke up. 'I can't

believe there was ever a fight. He's not a fighter, not physically. He's a coward. Always has been. He'd run a mile from a real fight.'

'How do you know that?' Samson asked quietly.

The silence which followed this question was as agonisingly mute as the death throes of a beached fish. It was broken by Ruddick. He turned towards Mary Coomber and in a voice laden with intimidation said, 'You told me.'

'Did I?'

'Yes, you did.'

'I don't remember saying that.'

'You did!'

She bowed her head, and she uncrossed her legs so that her knees could be tightly pressed together. It was the reaction of someone under threat who wished to withdraw into herself.

'Didn't you?' Ruddick persisted.

'Did I?' she replied.

'Yes. You said he was cowardly.'

'I may have said it wasn't very brave of him, when he lost his job, not to have come home and faced me with the fact. But I don't remember calling him a coward.'

'All right. All right. Your memory isn't reliable. We mustn't waste Mr Samson's time with what you can or can't remember.'

Samson intervened. 'Time is not wasted; it is spent. Like money it can be spent unproductively. Let's not be unproductive now. I'm not clear what useful purpose this meeting serves.'

'I wanted Mary to hear what you've found out,' said Ruddick. 'I want the facts made absolutely plain. When the thief crashed and was killed did or did not Coomber, quite deliberately and with cold calculation, plant evidence of his own identity on the thief's body and take upon himself the thief's identity?'

Samson took a deep breath before replying, 'I can't comment on states of mind.'

'It was a calculated deception engineered by a cowardly man trying to take advantage of someone's misfortune. And the deception would have continued indefinitely if he hadn't learned of Mary's inheritance. He is a conman, Mr Samson. You know it, and I know it, and I think that secretly Mary knows it although she won't admit it.'

Ruddick sat back as though he had just completed presenting the case for the prosecution.

Mary Coomber spoke. 'May I say something?' she asked, looking at Samson as though he were a presiding judge who could either give or withhold permission for defence counsel to make a statement.

'Please go ahead,' he said.

'Have you ever been sacked, Mr Samson, and faced the prospect of long-term unemployment?'

'Mary! Really!' Ruddick interjected.

'Please! Let me go on . . . Have you, Mr Samson?'

'No.'

'Then perhaps you wouldn't know how damaging it is to a man's self-esteem. He feels a failure. Some men can't face their loved ones after dismissal. Some even commit suicide.'

'I believe that is tragically true,' said Samson quietly.

'Is it then so very strange that when Colin saw the chance to adopt a new identity he seized upon it?'

Samson shook his head sadly. 'I can't comment on that, but it may have happened in the way you suggest.'

Ruddick stood up, swung round on Mary Coomber and snarled, 'I'm trying to protect your interests.'

She flinched. 'I know,' she said.

'Then don't ask stupid questions. I'll be in touch with you, Mr Samson. Come, Mary.'

That evening Shandy and Samson left the office together. It had been a fine day and the sun sinking in the west threw rays on to a thin strip of cloud making it an orange streak splashed on to a pale-blue palette. Shandy glanced at the sky and said, 'It's such a lovely evening I think I'll walk to Victoria. Get a breath of fresh air.'

'I could do with a bit of exercise. Mind if I come with you some of the way?'

'Of course not,' she said, falling into step beside him.

As they made their way through St James's Park Samson told her of the interview with Ruddick and Mary Coomber.

'You sound as though you can't stick the man.'

'He strikes me as a self-opinionated bully. I can't think what Mary C sees in him.'

'Maybe he has qualities you haven't seen.'

'Something doesn't add up,' said Samson, nimbly side-stepping half a dozen immaculately dressed Japanese, all festooned with cameras, 'he seems to know Coomber better than he lets on. He alleges it's merely hearsay, stuff he's learned from Mary, but I'm not so sure. And I'm not so sure how it's all going to end.'

'How do you mean?'

'Let's assume I get all the evidence Ruddick wants to show that Coomber is a liar and a self-seeking opportunist intent on fleecing his wife of her inheritance. And let's suppose he confronts her with unarguable proof. I'm not sure she'll take any notice. I think she may have already assessed the situation, looked at it from the worst viewpoint, and still decided she'll back him.'

'Maybe she loves him.'

'And Ruddick? Does she love him too?'

'Maybe. It's perfectly possible to love two people, or even more, at the same time. Not to be *in love*, that's different and usually excludes all others. But she could love both Ruddick and Coomber in different ways and for different reasons and it could lead to an awful conflict of loyalties. Poor woman. I feel sorry for her. But now it's my turn. I've heard about your problem case, now hear about mine.'

She told him about a young solicitor who had brought writs to be served and had promised to put a lot more work in her direction. 'The only snag,' she concluded, 'is that he seems to have developed a fixation on me. He gazes at me with adoring eyes.'

'You can cope, can't you?'

'I surely can. I've let him know I'm happily married and have a child. But . . . '

'But what?'

She smiled. 'Oh, nothing. I'll handle it. Aren't obsessives a pain.'

They said farewell at the exit gates and as Samson strolled back towards his apartment he was glad he had no emotional entanglements. Admittedly there were times when he felt lonely and depressed, and wondered what it would be like to share life with a caring partner, but these bleak moments passed.

As he was crossing the bridge which spanned the lake he paused and looked around. An old man was feeding sparrows and fat pigeons with broken bread rolls; young lovers, hands linked, were wandering across the park; a man with a laughing child on his shoulders was swaying from side to side pretending his burden was too heavy to carry. It was an evening when God seemed to be in his heaven and all was right with the world. Certainly it was all right with Samson's world. He was in reasonably good health, had plenty of money in the bank, and was free.

And then, quite unexpectedly, he was thinking of Mary Coomber and of the mischievous twinkle in her eyes when he had made a play on horsey proverbs, and how she had given the impression of gentle strength, and he wondered what it would be like to have a partner like her. Almost at once he was remembering how he had thought about Maureen Hislop while dining alone at Popjoy's Restaurant, and he recalled Shandy saying that what he needed was a good woman.

He resumed his walk. I don't need anyone, he said to himself, and for the time being he blotted out thoughts of having a partner with whom to share his life.

8

It wasn't in Samson's nature to disrupt routines simply to avoid unwanted encounters but he wished his early-morning walk didn't take him through Crown Passage. However, Ruddick's shop was closed and there was no sign of its owner. Samson went on his way glad to be spared of courtesy greetings or, worse, being buttonholed for an appointment. So far as he was concerned the Coomber case could rest for a while.

It didn't rest for long. At a quarter past eleven in the morning Georgia rang through on the intercom to say that Mrs Coomber had arrived and wanted urgently to see him. She was willing to wait until he was free. 'I can spare her a few minutes,' Samson said, 'bring her up.'

He gathered up some enlarged photographic prints which were scattered across the desk. The prints recorded an assignation between lovers and were required by a husband in a contested divorce case. The first print showed a woman climbing into a car within which could be seen the shadowy outline of a man's head. In other prints it seemed that the couple were embracing and the final picture showed the woman getting out of the car, her face clearly visible.

Samson shovelled the photos into a file cover a few moments before Mary Coomber entered the room. Her face was paler than on the previous day and in the absence of any make-up fine lines of premature ageing were visible. A bruise lay like a dark shadow beside her left eye. On being invited to sit down she went straight to the seat she had occupied less than twenty-four hours before.

'What brings you here?' Samson asked.

'I'm worried sick. It's Frank and Colin. I'm afraid something dreadful will happen.'

It was obvious that she was under considerable stress, so Samson immediately offered her the traditional British panacea.

'Would you like a cup of tea?'

The strain on her face eased. 'Oh, I'd love one.'

Samson leaned forward and pressed the intercom key. 'Georgia, tea for two, please. And I don't want any calls put through.' Having done what he could in the way of psychological first-aid he sat back, flicked on a switch which would activate a tape-recorder, and said, 'Now take your time. Tell me what's troubling you.'

'When we got home from seeing you yesterday Colin was waiting outside the house. My heart sank into my shoes. I knew there'd be trouble, and there was. Frank blew his top. It was terribly embarrassing. In the street, and within earshot of people waiting for a bus, he shouted, "What the hell are you doing here?" He isn't like that usually. Not in public. Normally in public he's very self-contained. I don't want to give you the wrong impression.' She paused. 'I don't want to be disloyal,' she added.

Samson gave a slight shrug but made no comment. In his opinion the only worthwhile loyalty was to one's own standards and beliefs. Other loyalties were too frequently the result of external influences operating on a susceptible conscience and these loyalties could be misguided and self-damaging.

After a moment's hesitation she went on, 'Colin said, "I want to talk to Mary. It's very important. Can we go indoors?" Frank looked furious but by now he could see the people at the bus-stop were listening. So we all went inside. They stood in the hall, arguing.' She lowered her eyes. 'Colin was saying, "She *is* my wife and this is *her* house. *You* are the intruder!" That was like a red rag to Frank. I thought it was

84

going to come to blows. I tried to intervene. I asked Colin what was important. He said that by a stroke of luck his agent had got a package lined up with an American company and was due to fly to Los Angeles tomorrow evening. That is, this evening. This man had got almost all the necessary finance but was just a hundred thousand light. Colin didn't get any further than that. Frank flung open the front door and manhandled him out.'

Georgia knocked and entered bearing a tray. She deposited it on a small table close to Mary Coomber, took a cup of tea to Samson and left the room.

'You say your husband was manhandled,' remarked Samson, continuing the interview. 'Didn't he offer any resistance?'

She shook her head. 'Colin is basically quite a gentle sort of man.'

'Was he always gentle to you?'

She looked surprised. 'Oh, yes. Always. Why do you ask?'

'I'm trying to form an opinion. Someone who is involved in putting together a video deal needs some self-assertiveness, even aggression.'

'He can be very assertive, but not by physical means.'

'It was certainly self-assertive to go on a dangerous chase when his car was stolen.'

She was silent.

'Has he got a quick temper?' Samson asked.

She thought before replying and when she spoke it was guardedly, as if she feared she might be caught out in a lie.

'He can get angry, but it is controlled anger.'

'And you are afraid that this anger might become uncontrolled, and Mr Ruddick's anger likewise?'

'That's it exactly.'

There were times in Samson's professional life when he knew that someone desperately needed sympathy and placatory reassurance, but that to provide this would be like giving a useless placebo to a sick person. 'I understand your concern and why you are worried, ' he said, 'but I'm not in a position to do anything about it, even if there was something I could do. I'm sorry, Mrs Coomber.'

She had an expressive face, sensitive as any cardiograph recording changes of heart movements, and her face registered a dip into despair. 'What can I say?' she asked plaintively.

'There's nothing to say. I can't allay your fears.'

'If only . . . ' she began, and paused.

'Yes?'

'If only I hadn't promised Frank not to mention something when we came here yesterday, I could talk about it now . . . I didn't sleep a wink last night . . . ' She fingered the bruise by her eye. 'He threatened me and he threatened to kill Colin if he came again asking for money.'

'I'm sorry, but this is purely a domestic matter and for the police if any violence occurs.'

'Yes, but . . . ' She looked anguished. 'If only I hadn't promised . . . '

Samson's curiosity was aroused and his compassion was touched. Using all his skill as an investigator, and his intuitive powers, he would try gently to draw out the information she was suppressing yet yearning to give.

'You promised him before you came to see me yesterday that there was something you wouldn't mention?'

She leaned forward. 'Yes.'

'I wonder if it concerns something which has slightly bothered me. The fact that Mr Ruddick seems to know more about your husband than he cares to admit.'

Her eyes lighted. 'Yes.'

'He knows your husband much better than he has admitted to me. I found it odd that he should insist, so strenuously and often, that what he knew of Mr Coomber was entirely based on hearsay. And yesterday, when he spoke of your husband always being a coward, it seemed as though he was speaking from first-hand knowledge.'

86

'Yes.' The monosyllable was uttered with all the encouraging eagerness of a child playing a guessing game which she wanted him to win.

'In fact, he has known him for a very long time indeed.'

'Yes.'

'If not all his life, then most of his life.'

'Yes.'

'Are they related?'

It was a crucial question but he knew what her reply would be before it was given. Her face had become transformed from despair to hope.

'Yes, you're right.'

'Don't let it trouble your conscience that you may have broken a promise,' said Samson. 'You haven't. You've told me nothing; I've told you. But now it's in the open, I'd like some details. Why are their surnames different?'

'That's because they're half-brothers. Frank's father died while he was a child and his mother remarried. It was someone called Charles Coomber. They had a son, Colin. Both parents are dead now but I remember Mr Coomber as very much the dominant partner in the marriage and he favoured Colin. Frank could do no right; Colin could do no wrong.'

'A recipe for fraternal jealousy,' remarked Samson. 'How did you meet Colin?'

'I was working as a receptionist for a medical practice and he was a rep for a pharmaceutical company. I felt sorry for him. Doctors get fed up with reps calling and being bombarded with literature about the latest drugs and none of the partners would ever see him. He persisted and one day, just before lunch, when he'd been turned down for the umpteenth time he said, "Cheer me up. Come out and have a bite to eat with me." And that's how it started.'

'You must have met his half-brother,' said Samson. 'Could you tell there was an enmity between the two?'

'I didn't see much of Frank. When I did, it was mainly at family gatherings such as Christmas. He struck me as being a lonely man. He seemed completely absorbed in collecting and selling militaria. That was his life. He didn't appear to have any time for women.' She flinched slightly as she added, 'Unlike Colin. The strange thing was that although they didn't get along with each other, Frank was best man at our wedding. On special occasions they managed to sink their differences. For example, at Christmas they always exchanged presents even though these weren't exactly thoughtful. Frank might give something from his shop and Colin would give a packet of blank video cassettes. He could get them at a cut price.'

'Has he always been keen on videos?'

'Yes. At least from the time that video recording became a commercial possibility.'

'Didn't he have any close friends? It does seem odd that he should ask a disliked half-brother to be his best man.'

'Colin travelled a lot and met other reps, but they weren't exactly his friends.'

'And after the "accident", in quotes, when you thought Colin was dead, did Mr Ruddick call on you?'

'He was at the cremation and very sympathetic. We met a few times for dinners out and he struck me as kind and thoughtful, and terribly lonely. I felt sorry for him. One night he invited me for a meal at his flat. It was a typical bachelor's place. Awfully untidy . . . '

'Just a moment,' Samson interrupted with a smile. 'I think I should tell you I am unmarried and my place is in good order, but perhaps I'm not typical.'

The pallor of her cheeks suddenly reddened as she blushed. 'Oh, I'm so sorry. I didn't mean to imply . . . '

Samson held up a silencing hand. 'Don't apologise. Please go on. You were talking about a meal at his flat. Did he prepare it himself?'

She gave a wry look. 'It was frozen food heated up in a microwave oven.'

'And it passed your mind that he needed a woman to look after him?'

She looked away. 'Maybe.'

'My assistant has similar thoughts about me,' said Samson. 'That's why I mentioned it. Am I right in thinking that after a while he moved in with you?'

'Yes. I sold my house and moved to Woodford to be nearer an aunt.' Her voice faltered and tears came to her eyes. 'She was a lovely person and her death so cruel. Anyway, she left me quite a bit in her will and so I gave up my job with the medical practice and took up unpaid voluntary work. Frank came to live at my house.'

'What sort of work?' Samson enquired.

'I'm with the Woman's Royal Voluntary Service.'

Samson nodded as though this was what he would have expected.

'I've heard a slightly different version of events from Mr Ruddick,' he said, 'not that it matters. The basic fact is that your husband returned from the dead and wants a substantial investment from you, and his half-brother who now shares your house resents this intrusion into his life.'

'That's right. After Colin had gone last night Frank was in a terrible rage and, as I've said, even threatened to kill him if he ever visited us again.'

'What I don't understand,' said Samson, 'is why he kept me in ignorance that he and Colin were half-brothers.'

'He's a private sort of person,' she said and she made the statement sound like a rueful apology. 'He doesn't like revealing too much of himself to anyone. Anyway, he didn't think it important. Apart from that, he thought it would seem rather strange to brief you to find out things which might be to the disadvantage of a close relative. I know there's nothing much you can do about all this, Mr Samson, but I just had to see someone, someone who I felt would understand. Frank is a man who has been full of repressed anger for a long time.'

'Are you frightened for your own safety?' Samson asked.

She gave a timid smile. 'A bit, I must admit.'

'That bruise by your eye – did he do it?'

She nodded her head.

'Why?'

'I told you that Frank manhandled Colin out of the house. Well, I called after him.'

'What did you call?'

'I called out that he could have the money.'

'And when Mr Ruddick got back into the house he hit you?'

Her 'Yes' was almost inaudible.

'I'm sure you know what options you have, but I'll spell them out. You can report the assault to the police. You can tell Mr Ruddick to leave your house. You can leave yourself, stay with a friend, and if necessary sell the house. Or you can do nothing and hope for the best.'

'I've thought of all those things. I can't turn Frank out. He sold his own place to be with me and before he left this morning he said how sorry he was for hitting me and he said I meant everything to him. There were tears in his eyes.'

'You are a soft touch, Mrs Coomber.'

'I am,' she replied in a surprisingly firm voice, 'but I'm not a push-over. I won't give in to him. Colin will have the money but I shall require some security. A written agreement that I have a share in any profits . . . I don't suppose that's the sort of thing you could do?'

'Unfortunately not. You need a lawyer who specialises in contract law. I'm sorry I can't be of more help.'

She stood up. 'I'm very grateful that you spared me your time. I feel more settled now.'

'Don't be bullied.'

'No, I won't.' She hesitated. 'I must pay you for this visit.'

'There's no charge.'

'It's very kind of you . . . You won't tell Frank I've been?'

'Of course not.'

He walked round the desk and shook her hand. She squeezed his hand slightly. 'Thank you so much,' she said.

After she had left he sat musing for a few moments.

There was, he suspected, behind a nervous and self-effacing exterior a woman who had inner strength and could exert an appealing influence.

Georgia came in to clear away the tea cups.

'Nice lady,' she remarked.

'Mrs Coomber?'

'Yes.'

'Why do you say that?'

Georgia thought for a moment. 'I don't know. She just is.'

9

It was three weeks later and while Samson was in New York at an international convention of private investigators that he heard of the death of Colin Coomber and the arrest of Frank Ruddick on a charge of murder. He had kept in daily contact with his office in London and it was from Shandy that he heard the news.

'How did it happen?' he asked.

It was a good line and the disbelief in her voice came through clearly. 'It sounds incredible. He didn't seem the type to commit murder, but it happened somewhere near the Excelsior Hotel in a passage called the Colonnade. Coomber's throat was cut.'

'Cut? With what?'

'This isn't public knowledge. The police are being very cagey but I've been in touch with Bernard. It was done with a *kukri*.'

'That's an Indian knife, isn't it?'

'That's right. It's used by the Gurkhas. A small *kukri* was found half a mile away. I think it may have come from Ruddick's shop but there were no prints on it.'

'Could it have been a mugging?'

'It isn't thought so. His wallet was still in his pocket. By the way, I've had Mary Coomber on the phone. She badly wants to see you as soon as you get back.'

'I'll be returning the day after tomorrow. Late flight. I shan't be home until midnight Thursday so fix an appointment for early on Friday.'

'Right. How are things?'

'Fine. Worth the visit. Drugs are still a talking point and DNA printing is another. Getting the dirt on politicians and other figures, character assassination, is a big money-earner. Industrial espionage is another winner. Yesterday we had an electronics man telling us about advances in the technique of sputtering windows with metallic film to reduce seepage of radio signals from computer terminals. And there's a lot of talk about ethics and image but it's all lip-service. We do nasty jobs for nasty people and don't choke on compunction. How are things with you?'

'Fine. Clockwork.'

'Good. I'll see you on Friday. You've got my number if you need me before then.'

Although Samson wasn't back in his apartment until after midnight he still went for his early-morning stroll round the park. On his way back through Crown Passage he noticed that the window of Ruddick's shop was screened with protective metal latticework. A board on the door read: 'These premises are closed until further notice'.

He was looking at the window when the tenant of the adjoining shop came out. He recognised Samson. 'Hard to believe, isn't it?' he said.

'Very hard,' said Samson.

'Such a quiet chap. You would never have thought.'

'You wouldn't,' replied Samson.

'But, as they say, there's a murderer in all of us,' the shopkeeper continued.

Samson raised eyebrows above his heavily lidded eyes. 'Is that what they say?' he enquired. 'I wonder if we should believe them.'

That was the end of the conversation. The shopkeeper went back into his shop.

Mary Coomber was at his office at ten o'clock. She was pale and drawn and her dark-blue eyes were like two bruises. She looked at Samson and he looked at her. 'It's a nightmare,' she said.

'Yes.' He pulled a chair forward. 'Sit down and tell me all about it.'

He took her arm and guided her to the chair. When he was seated behind his desk he said, 'Is he guilty?'

'I don't think so. That's why I'm here.'

'How strong is the case against him?'

'Very strong. The police found a note in Frank's writing among Colin's things at the hotel.'

'What did the note say?'

She felt in her handbag and gave Samson a piece of paper. 'This is a copy.'

Samson read the note. It said: 'Colin, you will stop at nothing to get hold of Mary's money. I will stop at nothing, and I mean nothing, to prevent you.'

He looked up. 'This is very circumstantial as evidence.'

'When the police confronted him with it he made a confession. It was written down and he signed it. He's retracted it now.'

'Why did he make a confession at all?'

'I don't know. I think he was temporarily out of his mind. I've asked him about it and he can't explain it. Apparently he said to the police, "The bastard deserved to die and I'd like to claim the credit." That statement was incorporated in the written confession. There was a bit more in it than that, but that was enough. That, and the note in his writing, and the knife which was of the sort that he sold. And evidence from Mrs Crowson.'

'Who is Mrs Crowson?'

'She's a neighbour. She heard every word when Frank chucked Colin out of the house including threats to kill. And he hasn't got an alibi for the night Colin was murdered. It happened at midnight and Frank wasn't at home.'

'Where was he?' Samson asked.

'He went for a drive. He was very disturbed. He was

frightened that he'd lost me and instead of coming home as usual he wanted to be alone to think.'

'Where did he go on this drive?' Samson asked.

'The M25. Just driving round the M25, driving and thinking.'

'No stops?'

'There's only one service station and he didn't stop at it. There's no one to say where he was.'

'He was lucky not to have had an accident or caused an accident,' remarked Samson. 'Motorways are no place for people to work out their emotional problems. And this drive was taking place at the time your husband was murdered?'

'Yes.'

'Why was he going on this dangerous round tour of London's orbital motorway? Why was he so disturbed?'

Mary Coomber became even more tense and her sad eyes were cast down, avoiding Samson's gaze. Her head became bowed.

'Why?' Samson repeated.

Her answer was in a whisper so quiet that he almost missed it.

'I'd spent the night before with Colin.'

She lifted her head as though it was weighed with leaden guilt.

'I suppose it might explain why a false confession was made. The man was past caring,' said Samson.

Her head drooped again and silence fell between them. When she looked up her eyes were beseeching; it was a look which implored him to understand her predicament. Samson gave her an encouraging smile. 'That was the other bit in Frank's confession,' she burst out. 'It finished, "He seduced my lady friend. He had it coming to him." ' A faint expression of amusement flickered across her strained face. 'It was typical of Frank to express it like that. Lady friend.'

Samson sat back and put his fingertips together so that

an arch was formed over his stomach, and when he spoke it was as if by putting fingertips together he was able to put facts together. 'Let me summarise the position,' he said. 'We have circumstantial evidence in the shape of a *kukri*, a witness to bad feeling between the two in the shape of a Mrs Crowson, lack of any sustainable alibi, a threatening note in writing, and a confession of guilt which was later withdrawn. On top of all that we have a motive as old as humanity and possibly older, sexual jealousy.'

Mary Coomber nodded her head.

'And you still think he is innocent?'

'I know Frank. He might do something in hot blood but he wouldn't be so calculating as to take a knife and lie in wait. And I know he doesn't like the sight of blood. A few weeks ago I cut my finger while I was slicing a cucumber. It bled quite a bit. He went white as a sheet and had to leave the kitchen.'

'I don't need to ask why you've come to see me,' said Samson. 'You want me to find evidence of innocence.'

'Yes,' she whispered.

'Does he have a lawyer?'

'Yes. Mr Goldstein. It was Mr Goldstein who got a copy of Frank's note to Colin and the confession which he withdrew. Mr Goldstein agreed that I should see you.'

Samson reached out to a shelf behind his desk and thumbed through the Law List. 'Mr S. Goldstein of Goldstein and Leverett of Wanstead?' he asked.

'Yes. A barrister is being briefed.'

'If I'm to take this on,' said Samson, 'there are some very personal questions I must ask.'

'I don't mind that.'

'I can see he had a motive but I don't know your motive for living with a man who hopes to marry you and spending the night with another.'

She sighed. 'Perhaps you won't understand. I hardly understand it myself. But to cut a long story short, I was due to meet Colin to discuss the film he wants to make and Frank said that if I went and met him I needn't bother to come back. I was furious. It takes a lot to make me furious, but he was telling me not to come back to my own house! Perhaps it's cowardly, but usually I take the line of least resistance. This time I didn't. I thought, "To hell with you!" . . . '

'You didn't say it,' Samson interrupted. 'You didn't say, "To hell with you." '

'No. But I thought it.'

'It might have been better if you'd said it. Cleared the air.' He paused. 'You told me that Mr Ruddick was full of repressed anger, but weren't you?'

She gave a rueful look. 'I suppose so. I didn't intend to stay out. It just happened. We had a good meal and I went back to Colin's room just for a last drink . . . God! Doesn't that sound corny!'

'It sounds human.'

'Colin can be a charmer. He has a way.'

'I daresay,' said Samson briskly. 'But what happened next? You went home the following morning, I assume?'

'Yes. Frank had already left for the shop. Then, very late, I think it was about nine in the evening I got a phone call from him. I asked if he was coming back and he said he needed time to think and was going for a drive.'

'But he came back eventually?'

'Yes, at about four in the morning. He looked terrible. He said he couldn't bear to lose me and if I wanted to have him share with Colin he'd be agreeable.' She hesitated. 'You could say that a reconciliation then took place.'

'How did the police get on to this?' Samson enquired.

'They found a card with the hotel's name and his room number in Colin's pocket. They searched the room and found papers about the film he wanted to make and my name and address. They called. I was shattered when they told me that Colin had been killed. But they didn't say how. They asked if I knew of anyone who might have a motive to kill him. I immediately thought of Frank but I didn't say anything. Anyway, I knew Frank would never do such a thing. I flannelled a bit and while I was talking one of the detectives noticed some daggers Frank had imported from abroad and not taken to the shop. They asked about these and I had to tell them that Frank dealt in militaria. I explained he had a shop and when they asked why the daggers weren't in the shop I said I wasn't sure. You see, sometimes he keeps things at the house. And then they asked if he ever dealt in replicas, objects smaller but just as lethal as the real thing. I didn't know at the time how Colin had been killed and I said he did. It was then they told me a replica *kukri* had been found with traces of blood on it.'

The account of her interview with the police left her looking exhausted, but the tension had gone from her body. She sat limply, pliable as a figure created from soft wax which had been dressed in clothes taken from some other waxwork effigy and which didn't quite fit her. Very slowly she pulled herself together and became a living person whose clothes fitted.

'Can you help me?' she asked.

'I shall try.'

'I'll pay whatever you ask.'

'We'll discuss fees some other time,' said Samson. 'Just leave everything with me. Where is Mr Ruddick at present?'

'Wormwood Scrubs. Remanded in custody. Do you want to see him?'

Samson shook his head. 'No. Not yet anyway.' He glanced down to check that the tape of their conversation was still running and then said, 'I've got one or two more questions.'

'Yes?' Her voice was eager. She leaned forward in her chair as if to grasp at a lifebelt.

'When Mr Ruddick returned at four in the morning after his motorway drive did you notice anything particular about his clothes?'

'No.'

'Were you able to see them closely?'

A blush coloured her pale cheeks. 'Yes. We, er,

embraced.' Her blush deepened. 'I was in bed, you see . . . He fell asleep in due course and I got up and tidied up his clothes which were on the floor. They were a bit creased but there was nothing particular about them. As a matter of fact, the police asked me the same question. They asked what he was wearing that night. I told them, and that because Frank was usually rather fussy about his clothes I'd taken his suit to the cleaners . . . Why are his clothes so important?'

'When the throat of a living creature is cut, lethally cut,' said Samson slowly, 'the blood will spurt out.'

He noticed a shiver run through her.

'It would be difficult to avoid some splashes on one's clothing,' he continued, 'unless one is very expert at that sort of operation and I'm certain Mr Ruddick is no expert. Can you tell me whether Colin was attacked from behind, taken completely unawares, or did he put up a fight?'

'Mr Goldstein has managed to find that out. It's thought he was attacked from behind. There was no evidence of a fight.'

'I believe this happened around midnight in a deserted passageway.'

'Yes.'

'How was the time established if nobody was about?'

'Colin's wristwatch was smashed when he fell. It stopped at two minutes past twelve.'

'Who discovered the body?'

'It was found shortly before one by a man who has a lock-up garage there.' She gave a little cough. 'My mouth is so dry, Mr Samson. Could I have a glass of water?'

'You certainly could. I'm sorry, I should have asked if you wanted anything to drink.' He keyed the intercom. 'Georgia, a glass of water, please.'

'I wonder . . . ' she began and stopped.

'Yes?'

'Could we have another window opened? It's silly but I'm feeling a little faint.'

99

Samson went and opened a window. Traffic noise from the street below which had been muted came through as though the volume had been turned up on a radio.

Georgia appeared with the water and left.

After Mary Coomber had taken a few sips of water Samson asked, 'Do you want to go on?'

'Yes . . . I shall be all right.'

For a few moments there was a silence between them. Mary Coomber took another drink. When Samson spoke it was to ask about the man who had put together a package for a video-film deal.

'His name is Henry Arzan.' She spelled the surname.

'And where was he at the time of the murder?'

A look of perplexity crossed her face. 'In Los Angeles, I expect. He flew there to finalise the deal.'

'Have you heard from him since?'

'No, but Colin had. When he took me out to dinner – the meal which caused all the trouble – he told me he'd heard that day. Henry had made a long-distance call and said that contracts were in the pipeline and he was staying on because he had another studio interested in a different project.'

'There's no reason, so far as you are aware, why he should wish your husband dead?'

'Absolutely none at all. They got along well together. It was quite a team. Different in personalities. Henry is very tough. A hard man, I would think. But he and Colin really hit it off.'

'Can you think of anyone who might have wished your husband dead?'

'No, I can't.'

'He had no enemies?'

'None that I know of. Of course, I don't know what might have happened while his memory had gone.'

'If indeed he ever did suffer amnesia.'

'Yes . . . You don't think Frank did it, do you?' Her question was a plea for reassurance.

100

'I have to keep an open mind,' replied Samson. 'That's not easy to do. I doubt if anyone possesses an open mind about things which concern them. Prejudices and preferences tend to plug up the most open of minds.'

'But Frank can't bear the sight of blood. He couldn't have used a knife.'

'Robespierre is reputed to have fainted at the sight of blood,' said Samson in the quietly firm voice of one who doesn't wish to provoke argument but knows it necessary to disabuse someone of a false premise, 'but that didn't stop him ordering blood-letting on a massive scale.'

She looked shocked. 'You don't think Frank ordered the murder, arranged for someone to kill Colin?'

'I have to keep an open mind. There's one more question I should like to ask. If you don't wish to answer I shall understand and not press the point. You seem to feel guilty about sleeping with your own husband.'

She gave a slight smile. 'I know what you mean. But I'm sick of deceits. I won't say more than that.'

Samson stood up. 'I needn't trouble you any more today but I'll be in touch.'

As they shook hands she looked up at him and said, 'I'm relying on you.'

'If Mr Ruddick is innocent,' he replied, 'I shan't let you down.'

10

It was six-thirty in the evening. Georgia had gone home and so had most office workers. The street, which had pullulated with life during the day, was almost empty of pedestrians although cars and taxi cabs were still making their way to and from St James's Square. Sometimes, after the office was closed, Shandy and Samson would discuss their cases. Today she came to his room.

'Care for a drink?' he asked.

'A dry Martini with ice would be just right.'

'I'll join you.'

'I had a nutter this afternoon,' said Shandy. 'She seemed to think our agency was a matrimonial agency. She began by saying, "You find people, don't you?" I said, "We try to." And then she said, "I'd like you to find me a wealthy Arab, an oil-rich sheikh." For a moment I wondered if it was a set-up for a *Candid Camera* stunt or, even worse, a video vengeance, but it turned out she genuinely wanted me to find her a rich Arab husband.'

Samson settled his portly frame on the side of his desk and looked with amusement at his chief assistant, friend, dietician and surrogate daughter, who was giving her perfectly manicured fingernail a critical scrutiny. He knew well enough that her sudden preoccupation with fingernails was a feigned distraction; she wanted him to ask, 'How did you deal with that one?'

'How did you deal with that one?' he asked.

'Easy. I said, "Go to Harrods, or Waitrose in the King's

Road, or the dialysis department at the London Clinic, and you'll find the sheikh of your desires." '

'Nice one,' said Samson with a laugh. 'You could have added the Dolder Grand Hotel in Zurich. When I was there last year there was an Arab, an emir I believe, who spent the whole day sitting in the reception lounge watching and being watched by other hotel guests.'

'If she comes back I'll tell her to go to Zurich,' said Shandy. 'How about your day?'

'Not bad. I had Mary Coomber in. She's really troubled.'

He gave a résumé of the interview and then said, 'I decided to have a look at the scene of the crime in the lunch hour.'

'What's it like?'

'The passageway is fairly wide, close to the Excelsior, but screened off by lock-up garages and high buildings. There's a pub at the corner called the Friend at Hand Tavern. I had a drink there and asked around but it's clear that there hadn't been any witnesses. The pub had closed for the night. The passageway is paved with cobbles. It has lights but they are spaced apart and, I'd imagine, not very strong. It looks a run-down patch. The lock-ups could do with a lick of paint, and rubbish-filled black dustbin liners don't improve the scene.'

'What do you think Coomber was doing there?'

'Your guess is as good as mine,' Samson replied.

'Do you think the creepy Ruddick did it?'

'I'm not sure, but I do know the police are set on making a case against him. During the afternoon I learned that they have found out that Coomber and Ruddick were half-brothers. What's more, their mother when she died left everything she had – it wasn't a lot – to Coomber. That can't have done anything for fraternal love.'

'What line are you going to follow?' asked Shandy, toying with an empty glass.

Samson noticed the movement and said, 'Let me get you another.' While he poured the drink he continued

103

speaking. 'Slitting throats isn't a typically British way of murder. If a knife is used it's usually for stabbing the body. There are exceptions. Annie Chapman, one of Jack the Ripper's victims, had her throat cut. But throat-cutting is more associated with suicide than murder. It's not an easy job, particularly if the victim puts up a struggle.'

Shandy took the replenished glass from him and seated herself on the chair earlier occupied by Mary Coomber.

'And suicide is ruled out?' she asked.

'Yes. As you know, the weapon was found.'

'Of course. The *kukri*.'

'Replica *kukri*. The real article weighs about four pounds and is two feet long. An interesting thing about the weapon is that there's a small protuberance near the handle which serves no apparent purpose. It stands at ninety degrees to the handle and is supposed to symbolise the penis.'

A smile stole across Shandy's face and she took a drink. 'Very symbolic,' she said. 'Sex and violence.'

'Funny you should use that phrase,' remarked Samson. 'The last time I heard it was when Ruddick was giving an opinion on what Coomber's video project would be like. He reckoned it would boil down to sex and violence under the gloss of classical myths. But I think you're right. I think there's a sexual dimension and I can think of someone who might have had a motive. The problem will be to get hard evidence.'

'Are you going to tell me who?'

'Wait until I've got something more to go on than instinct. I'll tell you then.'

'I suppose Mary Coomber could be a suspect,' said Shandy thoughtfully, 'but she seems too gentle a person.'

'I haven't dismissed her from my thoughts.'

'Except,' Shandy continued, 'women don't commit murder that way.'

'Don't they? What about Mary Eleanor Pearce, who cut the throat of her lover's wife? And the sixteen-year-old

104

Constance Kent, who almost decapitated her half-brother with a razor?'

Shandy flicked back a strand of hair which had fallen across her forehead. 'You've got me there. I'm not into criminology. Anyway, what next?'

'Next is something the police will probably already have done. Used the computer for other killings with a similar MO. Bernard still owes me a favour or two.'

Shandy finished her Martini. 'I must go, Paul will be waiting for his dinner, Kimberley for her bath, and I've got to buy something.'

'Go to Waitrose in the King's Road. A sheikh might buy it for you.'

She smiled. 'No way. I'm one of the rare ones, a happily married woman.'

The Two Chairmen in Dartmouth Street is a pub of some antiquity. Named after men who once bore a sedan chair on two poles, an illustration of this seventeenth- and eighteenth-century mode of transport appears on the façade of the pub. Its interior is furnished with bench seats and heavy round tables. An open fireplace faces a bar at the end of which is a smaller bar for the sale of snacks.

Samson arrived shortly after midday and ordered a pint of Guinness for Bernard and half a pint of lager for himself together with a bap filled with a thick slice of ham. He sat at a table from which he could view the entrance and within five minutes saw a familiar figure, fresh-faced and stockily built, wearing a nondescript greyish suit. The rendezvous was convenient for both men as it was roughly equidistant between Samson's office and New Scotland Yard.

'Morning, Bernard.'

'It's afternoon, John. Not like you to slip up on anything to do with time.'

Samson ignored the crack. 'I've lined up one for you,' he said, nodding towards the Guinness.

'Thanks. Cheers.' Bernard took a drink and then, looking

very directly at Samson, asked, 'And what else have you got lined up for me, or is this happy occasion simply because you like my witty conversation and want to hear the latest jokes going round the Yard?'

'There is something.'

'Thought as much. I should never have transferred to CID. Is it to do with the guy who nicks cars? What's his name? Vernon Brown?'

Samson shook his head. 'Nothing at all.'

'Then you won't be trying to con me into running something through the computer.'

'I was hoping for a small favour on those lines.'

'No favour is small, John, and you know it. Procedures have been tightened up. It's not easy any more.'

'Maybe it won't be necessary. Your lot may already have the info on file.'

Bernard gave a heavy sigh, took another draught of Guinness, and said, 'Let's have it. I still owe you for that job in Streatham.'

'It's the Coomber murder.'

Bernard gave a low whistle. 'That was nasty. How come you're interested?'

Before replying Samson shifted in his seat to allow a couple of middle-aged men, carrying tankards of beer, to pass by. The pub was now filling up, mostly with people working in nearby offices. When he was sure he wasn't being overheard Samson replied to Bernard's question.

'I've been retained by a very distant relative to find out what I can.'

'What's the interest of this relative – if there is a relative?'

Samson pretended to be shocked by the imputation that he might not be speaking the whitest of pure truths. 'How can you say such a thing! My client is a very old man with no involvement except that he fears for the family name and wants me to find out whether the charge will stick. Have you got any thoughts on that?'

'I'm not directly on the case but I know about it and

it'll take a good brief, the best, to get him off. The facts speak for themselves. Loads of motive, no alibi, one of his knives did the job . . . '

'One of his knives?' Samson interrupted.

'It's been established that he's the only importer of that make of *kukri* and has been for many years.'

'It could be a mail-order customer.'

'Come off it, John. You're clutching at straws. That suggestion has already been made but by an unfortunate accident some of his records of mail-order customers got destroyed.'

Samson took a last mouthful of bap and ham and said, 'Can I get you something to eat?'

'No, thanks. I'll have something to eat at the canteen later.'

'This accident when some mail-order records were destroyed – has it been checked out?'

'It's been checked. A temporary assistant at the shop put them in a dustbin by mistake.'

'What about the traceable customers?'

'All have been traced and all are still in possession of their nice little souvenirs of Indian culture.' Bernard glanced round to make sure their conversation was still private although there was now standing room only in the pub. 'And then there's his confession,' he said.

'Hasn't that been withdrawn?'

'Yes, but we went scrupulously by the book and he's an intelligent man, not some backstreet moron who can claim a low IQ and that police brutality made him confess. He's guilty, John, as guilty as you are for knocking back that lager. Can I get you another?'

'Not for me. What about you?'

Bernard shook his head. 'Not today. I'm due back. Shouldn't really be out. So, let's have it, what do you want?'

'The *modus operandi* – are there any other cases of throat-cutting still unsolved?'

'You're in luck. You are really a lucky man. I do happen to know we've run the computer on the MO angle and we've come up with one other case.'

'Who was that?' Samson's normally sleepy eyes were wide open as he waited for the reply.

'As I've told you, I'm not on the case. I don't know who. I only know there was one other found.'

'Could you . . . '

'Find out and let you know?'

'Yes.'

Bernard drained his glass of Guinness and stood up. 'Thanks for the drink, John. Nice to see you again. Can't remember a thing we talked about, can you? Anyway I'll give you a bell some time.'

'You've got the number of my apartment as well as the office?'

'I have. How do you like your new patch?'

'Very much.'

'I liked it better when you were in SE whatever. You were a helpful ear in a dodgy area.'

'I still contribute to the PD charity.'

Bernard smiled. 'I'm sure my widow and kids will appreciate that. See you.'

He turned and seemed to merge into a crowd of drinkers; one second he was there and the next he had vanished.

Later that afternoon Samson telephoned Mary Coomber. He said there was a question he had omitted to ask – did Mr Ruddick ever employ an assistant?

'He did for a while a few months ago,' she said, 'but she was pretty useless. Frank went to the Far East – India and Japan – to line up suppliers. He needed someone to look after the shop. I couldn't do it all the time. I managed part of the time and Beryl took over when I wasn't there. But she was one of those people who have an urge to make everything clean and tidy and one day she got rid of a lot of old magazines and papers. Admittedly most were of no use. There was junk mail Frank had clung on to – he's a bit of a hoarder – but she overdid the tidying up. She got rid of a list of some of the customers. Frank was absolutely furious when he got back, and fired her on the spot.'

'This assistant, Beryl,' he said. 'How did Mr Ruddick come to employ her?'

'She answered an advert in the *Evening Standard*. Frank got three replies and she seemed the most suitable. She was a student of oriental languages at London University and wanted a job during the vacation . . . Is it important?'

'No. I can "eliminate her from my enquiries" as my brothers in blue would say.'

It was a brother in blue who gave him a call that evening at his apartment.

'I've got the details of that case, John.'

'I'm listening agog.'

'Name: Daisy Jane Simkins. Age: eighty-one. Lived alone in large detached house in Theydon Bois, Essex. Motive seems to have been burglary; the house was turned upside down. The old girl was in bed at the time. The case is still open and I daresay it'll be looked at again although it's hard to see a connection apart from the MO between an old woman in Theydon Bois, which is up-market, and a much younger man in a London passageway.'

'How long ago was the woman killed and was she a widow?'

'It was June. The twelfth. Quite widely reported. She was what used to be called a spinster.'

Samson thought for a moment. 'I don't remember it, but I was abroad at the time.'

'The media coverage soon faded.'

'No sexual element?'

'None at all. That might have kept the story alive a bit longer.'

'Was much taken from the house?'

'Some silver, a portable TV, but nothing much more.

She was rich but had simple tastes. Her real valuables were in a bank safe-deposit box.'

'No sightings of an intruder?'

'None at all. The house is set back from a side road and there are bushes all around.'

'Who stood to benefit from the death?'

'You want to know a lot, don't you,' said Bernard, a grudging note in his voice. 'I'm not sure who benefited. I think it was a niece. A niece identified the body and arranged for the funeral. I'm speaking from memory but I know she was ruled out from our enquiries.'

'Thanks, Bernard. It's been a help.'

'Glad to hear it.' A chuckle came into Bernard's voice as he added, 'I'm sure this elderly relative you represent, and who's worried about the family's name being tarnished, will be most interested to learn all the facts about the death of an aged spinster in Theydon Bois.'

Samson wasn't to be drawn by ribbing sarcasm. He said, 'By the way, how's the new arrival? I forgot to ask when we met.'

'Mother and baby are both doing well, I'm happy to say.'

'Great. Thanks, again. Bye.'

Before the call Samson had been half-drowsing, half-listening, to a radio concert. He stood up and for a few moments looked strangely irresolute like someone who has forgotten what he intended to do next and is caught in a no-man's land of mental blockage. Then he moved purposefully across the sitting room, past a walnut cabinet on top of which stood a blue Murano goblet, and to a glass-fronted bookcase. After sliding across a panel he reached down and selected an A–Z road map which showed an area within a thirty-five-mile radius of London.

Theydon Bois was roughly eight miles from Woodford Green where Mary Coomber lived and easily reached by a road running through Epping Forest. He put away the road map and returned to an armchair next to which was a telephone, a glass of whisky, and a notepad and pen.

The radio was playing Beethoven's sonata for pianoforte in E flat but Samson wasn't listening; he was debating whether to call Mary Coomber again. She had inherited the estate of a rich aunt and the inheritance had been within the past year or so. Was it possible that she was the niece of the woman who had been murdered in Theydon Bois? If so, it would be another nail in the prosecution case against Frank Ruddick. It could be alleged that he killed, or hired a contract killer to murder, the aunt so that the woman he hoped to marry would inherit and then, when it seemed as though the inheritance might pass to his half-brother, he had killed the half-brother.

If CID at New Scotland Yard weren't already aware of this angle they soon would be if they were on the ball and, in Samson's opinion, they were tenacious ball-players.

He picked up the handset and keyed Mary Coomber's number.

After the ninth ring, and just as he was about to give up, she answered.

'Samson here, Mrs Coomber. I'm sorry to trouble you again.'

Her 'Hello' had been cautious but her 'That's all right' was warm. Samson, detecting the change of tone, asked, 'Are you being bothered by unwanted calls?'

'There have been some from the bottom end of the tabloids once they discovered Colin was married to me. That's why I didn't answer at once.'

'I've got another question for you.'

'Yes?'

'Didn't you say you'd moved to Woodford Green to be near an aunt?'

'Yes. She was old, not very strong, but very independent. I was able to visit her daily.'

'What was her name?'

Mary Coomber gave a nervous laugh. 'Why do you want to know?'

'Was it Daisy Jane Simkins?'

Samson heard a faint gasp and then, 'How did you know?'

'When Mr Ruddick came to see me and ask me to obtain evidence that your husband hadn't really suffered amnesia he mentioned that your aunt had left you a lot of money but he didn't say she had been murdered. He simply said she had died.'

The silence following this remark was so prolonged that Samson wondered if there had been a break in the connection. 'Are you still there?' he asked.

'Yes. Frank can be a very secretive man. He doesn't like to give away more than he has to. It's his character.'

'The character of a hoarder. You called him a bit of a hoarder.'

'That's right. I know what you must be thinking. Frank could have done away with Auntie Daisy so that I would inherit her money and then, when Colin reappeared, he got rid of him too. But that isn't the case. I'm sure he didn't do it.'

'You may be sure, but would the police be so sure if they make the connection?'

Another silence and then she said, 'It doesn't look so good, does it?'

'No. Not unless I can find someone who fits even better than Mr Ruddick.'

'I hope you will. I know Frank is a difficult man but he needs me, now more than ever before.'

In his observations on human behaviour Samson had come to the conclusion that possibly by some sort of biological programme most women needed to be needed. Men didn't need to be needed quite as much as women did. Not that he would have said as much to Shandy, who would have squashed his assertion by saying biology had nothing to do with it. She would have said that in a male-dominated society women had to fulfil men's needs and that was why they needed to be needed.

Mary Coomber broke a long silence by saying, 'Have you any ideas on who killed Colin?'

'It's a long shot but I do have one idea. The difficulty will be in proving what I think.'

Her voice became clearer, sharper, as she said, 'Who do you think?'

'Trust me, Mrs Coomber. I'll do my best. And now, why don't you take your phone off the hook?'

'I think I will . . . I feel so tired . . . Thank you for all you're doing, Mr Samson.'

Before retiring for the night Samson folded a fifty-pound banknote and slipped it into an envelope with the brief scribbled message, 'A christening present.'

On the envelope he wrote Bernard's home address.

He was a light sleeper and on those nights when he went to bed with an unsolved problem teasing his mind it wasn't unusual for him to stay awake until three or four in the morning. Sometimes to break the cycle of recurrent but dead-end ideas he would make a cup of tea and go to the sitting room and sit for a while in his favourite armchair. He would then tackle *The Times* crossword puzzle in the hope that by a different form of mental exercise he would achieve rest from the besetting problem. He regarded it as cerebral homeopathy.

But tonight the crossword defeated him and, what was worse, gave him no respite from the question which went round and round in his head like a cat chasing its tail. If Frank Ruddick was innocent of murdering his half-brother, who was guilty? Who, apart from Ruddick, disliked Coomber enough to murder him? Was it possible that someone who knew him better as Vernon Brown had been motivated to kill him? Could the murder be pinned on the part-owner of a guest house in Bath?

Freddie Hislop had reason to dislike Vernon Brown but, having got rid of him, why should he pursue him to London? And how could he find where his quarry was living unless

113

he'd come across evidence that his wife was still in contact with the originator of video vengeances?

It was a long shot that Hislop was the killer but it was the only shot Samson possessed. And even if he was the killer how could it be proved in a way that would satisfy a jury?

He finished his cup of tea and went back to bed.

11

Owing to other commitments it wasn't until three days after his meeting with Bernard that Samson was free to drive to Bath. He parked his car in a side road near Pinetree Guest House.

As he walked up the path leading to the house he noticed the lawn was as green and well mown as when he'd last seen it. He rang the door-bell and after a few moments the door was opened by Maureen Hislop. The expression on her face changed from welcoming warmth to dismay. She looked at Samson as though he was a bailiff come to seize all her goods and chattels. 'It's you,' she said. It wasn't the reception he had expected. 'We haven't got a room vacant if that's what you want,' she went on.

'No room at all?'

'We're getting very busy. Time of year. Sorry.'

She was about to close the door when a voice called, 'Who is it, Maureen?'

She hesitated before calling back, 'It's Mr Dan.'

Seconds later Freddie Hislop appeared. 'What can we do for you, Mr Dan?'

'I was hoping you'd have a room available but apparently you haven't.'

'Come down to buy some more clocks, have you?'

'I'm here on business, yes.'

'Well, we are fairly fully booked. We're not a large house. But I think I might just be able to accommodate you. We don't have any rooms spare but when it's an old

115

and trusted customer I sometimes give up my room and sleep on a sofa-bed in our private room. It won't take a minute to change the sheets if you'd care for the use of my room.'

Completely nonplussed by this offer, Maureen Hislop looked at her husband and then at Samson as though they were speaking a language she was at a loss to understand.

'I don't want to put you to any trouble,' said Samson.

In saying this he was balancing the risk of having the offer withdrawn against the appearance of being over-eager to accept. He very much wanted the room, any room, in the house if he was to succeed in proving Hislop either guilty or innocent of the murder of Colin Coomber. For a fragile moment he thought the gamble of being polite at the expense of being grasping was going to fail. Hislop's pointed face seemed to contract with doubt but it expanded again in a strange smile.

'It won't be any trouble, Mr Dan. It's nice to see you again. The terms will be just the same although my bedroom has an *en suite* bathroom, not the last word in bathrooms perhaps but better than the facilities you had before. How long will you be staying?'

It puzzled Samson why Hislop's small close-set eyes had begun to burn with an inner excitement and why Maureen had been so unwelcoming.

'I'm not sure, one night or two,' he said.

'I suppose that depends on how well your business goes.'

'Yes.'

'Well, you can stay as long as you like. I'm sure Maureen will look after your every need.' He gave his wife a poke in the ribs. 'Won't you, my dear?'

'Of course.' She forced a smile.

'You don't seem to have any luggage with you, Mr Dan,' said Hislop.

'I've left it in the car.'

'Maybe I should show you the room first and then if you like you can move in.'

Hislop stood back to allow Samson to enter.

116

They went up narrow staircases to the top floor. Hislop threw open a door. 'Here it is. Not palatial, but the bed is comfortable. All the beds are. We're very keen on that. Good beds make happy guests is our motto.'

The room was dominated by a king-sized bed covered by an orange eiderdown. The curtains were deep red and the carpet a faded yellow. The wallpaper was of cabbage roses, which looked as if they had been grown with the aid of a wonder fertiliser, on a pale-blue background.

'Maureen's room is just opposite,' said Hislop. 'These are the only rooms on this floor. You won't be troubled by noise from the other guests. It's very private. Just you and Maureen.'

'It's kind of you to let me have the room.'

'Well then, if you'd like to get your bags you can move in. I'll see the sheets are changed. Oh, I'd better take my pyjamas.' He gave a squeaky laugh, 'I don't suppose you want to borrow them. It might be confusing.'

'And a tight fit for me,' responded Samson.

Hislop reached under the pillow and took out a pair of striped blue and white pyjamas.

'I'm so glad you liked our humble abode enough to return,' he said. 'We do our best to make our guests as comfortable as possible.'

'And you succeed,' said Samson. 'I'll go and get my overnight bag.'

On his return from the car, and on his way upstairs, he had a quick look inside the room he had previously occupied. It seemed unused. A fresh bar of soap lay on the washbasin and there was no sign of a toothbrush, any other toiletries or any luggage. The bed was made up. Why, he wondered, had Maureen Hislop said that no room was available, and why had Hislop been so willing to loan his own bedroom? Samson had the feeling he was being set up, but for what purpose he didn't know.

Whenever he travelled he took a few compact technological aids and these included a hand-sized radio-frequency detector. It resembled a television remote-control transmitter and had a short retractable aerial. Samson took this piece of counter-surveillance equipment from his overnight bag and began sweeping the room for electronic devices. He found one secreted by the bed-head. Was Hislop in the habit of lending his room to any strange male in the hope of bugging pillow talk?

Samson put the detector away and made a visual search. A wardrobe and chest of drawers held an assortment of clothes but there was nothing unusual to be found. He did, however, notice that the light bulbs in the two bedside lamps and an overhead light were of an unusually high wattage.

Before leaving the room he double-locked the overnight bag.

All guests at Pinetree were provided with a key to the front door. After his evening meal Samson let himself into the house. He had decided to order a whisky and was about to press the bell-push in the reception hall when Hislop appeared.

'Ah, Mr Dan. Back again. I hope you've had a productive time.'

'All Time is productive. Without Time none of us would be here.'

'Pardon?'

'It doesn't matter. Could I have a whisky brought to my room?'

'Certainly. When you were here before you had Black Label. Same again?'

'You have a good memory.'

'In this business it pays to remember the preferences of guests.' Hislop gave a meaning smirk. 'Every preference,' he added.

'I'd like Black Label with an equal measure of mineral water, Scottish water for preference.'

'You shall have it, sir.'

The reply was polite but the look which accompanied it

was arrogant and knowing. Hislop appeared in the bedroom a few minutes later carrying a tray. 'We don't have Scottish water,' he said. 'Will Malvern do?'

Samson nodded and after putting down the tray Hislop poured a measure of water. Without looking at Samson he asked, 'How's business, Mr Dan?'

'Pretty good.'

'There should always be a market for clocks. People need to tell the time.'

'They do. But they seldom listen to what Time has to tell them, or why are so many deaths caused through physical over-exertion by the over-fifties?'

Hislop presented the tray to Samson, who took his drink from it.

'That is a profound remark, Mr Dan. But it doesn't apply to all of us. I flatter myself that I am exceptionally fit for my age and I intend to live to be a hundred.'

Samson raised his glass. 'To your century,' he said. 'Of course a lot depends on genetics and a healthy life-style.'

'So they say,' Hislop replied. 'So they say,' he repeated, and then quoting Samson, 'but they seldom listen to what Time has to say to them. That remark was very profound.'

A hint of mockery in this reply wasn't lost on Samson, who changed the subject. 'I expect your business here prevents you from having many holidays or leaving the premises very often.'

Hislop's close-set eyes narrowed. 'You're right. I'm tied to the business. Can't get away. Maureen has talents but she couldn't manage this business on her own.'

'Don't you ever get away?'

Hislop paused before answering. 'Hardly ever . . . I hope you'll be comfortable, Mr Dan.' He glanced round the room. 'It isn't the best bedroom in the house. That belongs to Maureen. But it has TV and radio. Not every room has that.'

'It's good of you to sacrifice your bedroom.'

'No sacrifice, Mr Dan. I've done it before when I've

taken a liking to a guest, and Maureen likes him too. I don't keep anything private in here, but you may have realised that already.'

He smirked and Samson had the feeling he was being baited, and that Hislop knew he'd checked out the room.

'Will you be needing anything else?' Hislop asked. 'Anything at all?'

'I don't think so.'

'No early-morning call?'

'No, thanks.'

'Well, if there's anything you need during the night Maureen is close at hand. She won't mind being woken up if she's asleep. She'll provide anything you want.'

'I'll bear it in mind.'

Hislop picked up the tray. 'I must be on my way. Leave you to enjoy your drink in peace. I'll wish you good night.'

On his own, Samson switched on the television but he paid little interest to the programme. Instead, he tried to figure out how Hislop could have known the room had been searched. He got up from his chair and prowled around. It wasn't until he went into the bathroom that he understood. The bathroom wasn't the same length as the bedroom and in the bedroom's extra space there was a wall mirror.

Back in the bedroom he switched off the TV and cautiously opened the door. Nobody was in sight. At the end of a short landing was what looked like an airing cupboard. Samson went to it and found it locked. Within two minutes the key gun had opened the door. Samson entered a small closet which was bare except for mirrors on two of the walls. He went to one of the mirrors, looked in it and had a perfect view of his bedroom. The other mirror showed the interior of Maureen Hislop's room, a dainty boudoir of fuschia pinks and mauves. Everything which could be embellished with frills was frilled, and the wide double bed looked like an iced cake covered in pink froth. The wallpaper was covered with heart-shaped motifs and the overall impression was of a three-dimensional Valentine card.

After locking the closet door Samson returned to his room. During the time that he'd been out for an evening meal his bed had been turned back ready for when he retired for the night. The sheets and pillow slips were clean and fresh. He was thinking about the difference of decor in the two bedrooms, the difference between consonance and dissonance, when he noticed something he hadn't observed before. Projecting between two pillows like a tiny tongue sticking out from enormous white lips was a pink envelope. He extracted it; the name 'Mr Dan' was written on the cover.

He ripped open the envelope and took out a piece of pink notepaper which had the simpering 'Love Is' boy and girl characters printed at the bottom. The note, written in a hand he had seen before, read: 'When I come to ask about breakfast and any extras please turn me down. Watch what you say. Your life depends on it. Meet me at Binks Restaurant near the Abbey and opposite the Roman Baths at 11.00 tomorrow morning and I will explain. Very sincerely, Maureen. P.S. Keep your door locked.'

12

Samson put the note in his pocket and sat on the side of the bed looking straight at the mirror. Sooner or later Hislop would be on the other side staring at him. It was clear that the system operated by the couple was for Maureen to come late to the room of a single male to ask what he would like for breakfast. She might apologise for not having asked this question earlier. She would probably be wearing a negligée which she might touch or play with suggestively, and she would give other hints and indications that her guest's pleasure would be her pleasure. Unless there were two-way mirrors in other bedrooms she would, if her ploy succeeded, invite the guest to her or her husband's bedroom. In the meanwhile Hislop would have stationed himself in the closet hoping to view some action. But what was his purpose? Was it merely voyeuristic gratification or was the motive more sinister, such as blackmail?

It was while he was pondering on motive that there was a light tap on the door.

'Come in,' he called.

Maureen Hislop entered. She was wearing a pink satin dressing gown and pink sling-back sandals. 'I'm sorry to disturb you, Mr Dan,' she said, 'but I completely forgot to ask what you'd like for breakfast. As you know, I can do a full English breakfast or just fruit juice, tea or coffee, and rolls. Would you like the full English breakfast again?'

Samson stood up and interposed himself between her and the two-way mirror. 'Full English breakfast, please.'

She moved towards him and stood close. 'Nothing else?' she asked, and she loosened the girdle of her dressing gown. The movement wafted the scent of a heavy perfume in Samson's direction. 'Isn't there anything else you want?' she asked. 'Don't you feel a bit lonely in here on your own?'

'I like my own company.'

It was a new experience for Samson to be at the wrong end of a surveillance operation and he didn't care for it.

Maureen Hislop moved even closer so that her dressing gown almost brushed against his trousers. 'It's not right for a man to be lonely if there's a woman willing to keep him company,' she said, and as she spoke she glanced towards the bed to see whether her note had been removed. She gave a little smile and Samson, still with his back to the two-way mirror, winked at her.

'Don't worry about Freddie,' she said, loosening the dressing gown so that it fell open revealing that she was wearing nothing underneath but a pair of black lace panties. She took his hand and steered him towards the bed. If Hislop was watching he would now see everything.

Samson pulled his hand away. 'You're wasting your talents,' he said. 'I'm not interested.'

'You're not the other sort, are you?'

'Other sort? What other sort?'

'Well, you know, sort of gay.'

'No, I'm not sort of gay.'

'Good. Mind you, I've got nothing against gays. They're often nicer people than the straights, but they aren't any use to a hot-blooded woman.' She twined her arms round Samson's neck. 'Kiss me.'

'Are you a maiden aunt?' Samson asked.

She smothered a laugh. 'No. Why?'

'I only kiss maiden aunts and only on Thursdays.'

She tried to kiss him but he gently pushed her away.

'Don't you want anything?' she asked. 'I can give a nice massage.'

'I'm allergic to massages,' Samson replied. 'My doctor tells me it's something to do with skin sensitivity. I come out in a rash if anyone touches me.'

'All right then. I can do better than that. I can give you what every man wants but is usually too nervous to ask for.'

'What's that?' asked Samson, genuinely interested.

'You know the advert on TV where a woman eats a banana?'

'Yes.'

'That.'

'I haven't got a banana here,' said Samson ingenuously. 'I'd love to see you eating a banana but I'm afraid I didn't equip myself with a banana before I came here.'

She almost burst out laughing and Samson was beginning to enjoy the situation.

'Warm in here, isn't it?' she asked, and without waiting for his reply she slipped off her dressing gown and let it drop on to the floor. 'The moment I saw you,' she said, 'I knew you were a real man. If I flirted with you a bit it was because I was falling in love with you.'

Samson took a pace back and surveyed her as though appraising an *objet d'art*. 'If I was an artist,' he said, 'I'd like to paint you, but I'm a humble dealer in rare and antique timepieces. And, to be honest, your piece doesn't interest me in the least.'

She pretended to be indignant. 'In that case,' she said, 'you can go to bed with your bloody timepieces,' and snatching up her discarded dressing gown she stormed from the room.

Samson felt like making a two-fingered gesture at the mirror but he resisted the impulse. He also felt like darting outside to catch Hislop leaving the closet but he resisted this temptation too. It could prejudice the meeting next day suggested by Maureen.

At one period in his life Samson's bedtime reading had been science fiction. After this phase he had a spell of

124

reading learned journals as a deliberate exercise in self-education but this palled when Shandy took an Open University course in literature and, perversely perhaps, he took the view that formal education was over-rated. Like religion, formal education had much to answer for; the only worthwhile university was the university of life, the only worthwhile religion was the religion of agnosticism. This phase also passed. Now for bedtime reading he had reverted to Charles Dickens, a childhood favourite. Although the consensus of opinion among Dickensian scholars and critics was that *A Tale of Two Cities* didn't rank among his best works Samson preferred it to all others. Not only did he like the story but he suspected that the book contained a disguised self-portrait; Charles Darnay and Sidney Carton were the two sides of the author's character.

It was shortly before midnight, and just as he was about to put the book down, that he heard a tap on the door. He climbed out of bed and unlocked it. Maureen Hislop stood outside wearing nothing but the pink satin dressing gown which hung open. Her mouth smiled but her eyes were clouded with anxiety.

'I could see your light was on,' she said, 'and I was wondering if you needed company. And I came to say I'm sorry if I was rude to you. I didn't mean it. I'm sorry.'

'That's all right,' said Samson.

But it wasn't all right. The intrusion was obviously a put-up job directed by Hislop.

'I get lonely at night too,' she said. 'Freddie never gives me a cuddle, let alone anything else.'

'And nor shall I,' said Samson firmly. 'Unless you leave immediately I shall report this incident to the police tomorrow and lodge a complaint against you for importuning.'

She closed the dressing gown and tied its girdle. 'I'm sorry. I didn't mean to disturb you.'

'Go back to your own room.'

Her smile became genuine. 'If that's what you want.'

'I do, and think yourself lucky that I shan't make a complaint provided you go now.'

She obliged his request, and in a hurry.

Samson locked the door again, returned to bed, and switched off the light. He felt sure that Hislop wanted to catch him in bed with Maureen. He might even film the scene from the closet. Any sort of photographic record could be used as blackmail, and it could be employed in discrediting him should there ever be a criminal prosecution against Hislop. A skilled advocate for the defence would try to persuade a jury not to rely on the evidence of a man who had seduced the defendant's wife.

It was some time before he fell asleep.

Samson came down for breakfast. Only two others were in the dining room. Sitting at separate tables, papers spread beside their plates, they had the morning-clean looks of company reps.

Maureen Hislop brought his breakfast. She was unsmiling and looked tired. Apart from saying, 'Enjoy your meal,' she didn't speak.

Hislop was in the hall when Samson, carrying his overnight bag, came downstairs to check out.

'I hope you slept well, Mr Dan.'

'Very well, thanks.'

As he presented the bill Hislop said, 'Are you going back home today or have you more business in our fair city?'

'I have some business.'

'Ah. Well, if your business should delay you, you would be very welcome here. There should be a vacancy tonight.'

'I'll bear it in mind.'

'I trust you found my bed comfortable.'

Samson counted out some banknotes. 'Very comfortable, thanks.'

Hislop gave Samson a curious look and, lowering his voice, said, 'I believe Maureen disturbed you during the night. I'm sorry about that. Her trouble is that she wants to provide every comfort even when it's not needed or appreciated. She can be over-friendly sometimes.'

'To a ship that's passing in the night?'

'Exactly.'

'But if the ship doesn't pass, it can run the risk of being sunk,' said Samson, pocketing the receipted bill.

Hislop recoiled slightly. 'Sorry, I don't get you.'

'Just a play on words,' smiled Samson. 'Good day.'

Samson's childhood had mostly been spent in a tough part of London's East End. This had been followed by a spell as a rating in the Royal Navy and one or two dead-end jobs until he had inherited a debt-collecting agency from an uncle. He had built up the agency into a prosperous private investigation agency but, apart from an interest in clocks which had given him fleeting insights into past social history and so-called gracious living, he had little aesthetic appreciation.

With increasing maturity his attitudes had changed from a defiant philistinism to a dawning pleasure in the fine arts, particularly the greater arts of painting, architecture and music; he also developed a liking for the lesser arts of acting and ballet.

Having time to spare before meeting Maureen Hislop he decided to savour the beauty of Bath and he took a stroll through the city. It was a morning of bright sunlight which gave a subtle glow to the mellowed façades of Georgian buildings and a sparkle to the River Avon.

Shortly before eleven he passed though a colonnade in Stall Street and entered a paved precinct in front of the abbey church. The small square was crowded with visitors, some in shorts and vivid T-shirts, some in more formal dress, and a few in way-out gear which advertised independence from any convention except the convention of wanting to be seen to be different. Included in the last group Samson noticed a young man wearing greasy rags. He had a Sioux haircut and his bare arms were heavily tattooed. Walking a pace behind him was a young woman with lank uncombed hair who looked as though she had slept rough for many weeks without benefit of hygiene.

Samson stood and surveyed the busy scene in which denizens of the twentieth century mingled in changing patterns against a static but dignified backdrop from earlier centuries. To his right was the eighteenth-century Pump Room constructed of honey-coloured limestone; ahead was the abbey, its façade intricately worked in stone to depict the vision of a heavenly ladder; and to his left was Binks Restaurant fronted by three rows of white plastic chairs and tables. Most of the tables were occupied but after entering the restaurant for a self-service cup of coffee Samson seated himself at a vacant table and waited for Maureen Hislop. It was five minutes to eleven.

By ten past eleven his coffee was finished and there was no sign of her. He wanted another drink but as every table was now occupied and people were searching for a space to sit he didn't want to risk losing his vantage point.

Three young men, heads shaven, the backs of their coats painted with the logo of anarchism, cut their way like a swathe through a party of babbling schoolchildren. Samson glanced at his wristwatch. It was now twenty-three minutes past eleven. He was about to leave when he saw her threading her way through the party of schoolchildren, who were leaving the precinct. Her face was flushed and she looked flustered. Pausing, she gazed round the tables outside the restaurant.

Samson stood up and raised an arm. She gave a brief smile and hurried towards him.

13

'Sorry I'm late,' she said breathlessly.

'Let me get you a coffee.'

'No, thanks. I can't stay long and I've got a lot of shopping to do.' She dropped an empty orange shopping bag and a handbag by a white plastic seat and sat down. 'I don't know what's got into him. I think he suspects something. He's a cunning sod. Pardon the language. I was afraid you might have gone.'

'And I was afraid you weren't going to turn up. Were you delayed?'

'He knows I usually go out at half ten for provisions but today he kept me talking and doing things. It was as if he knew I wanted to be away and was purposely frustrating me. He can be very cruel, Mr Dan.' She gave him a searching look and then, 'That's not your real name, is it?'

Samson shifted as though his chair had become uncomfortable but his voice didn't correspond with the body movement. He sounded at ease and relaxed when he said, 'What on earth makes you think that?'

'It was the photo of Colin you said you'd found under your bed the last time you were here. Freddie knew Colin had never used that room. He didn't believe you.' She lowered her voice. 'Someone in the police was able to trace your car number and give him your name and address.'

Samson knew that others in his profession had helpful friends in the police force but surely Hislop's contact didn't owe him a professional favour.

'Your husband has a police contact who'll risk a severe reprimand or even dismissal to provide him with confidential information?'

Her voice remained muted. 'Yes,' she whispered.

'And the policeman isn't a close relative or a close boyhood chum?'

'No.'

'And he doesn't owe your husband a very great favour?'

Almost inaudibly she replied, 'No.'

'Would I be right in thinking your husband has something on this policeman, something of which he would be ashamed?'

'Yes.'

'He is married, this policeman?'

'Yes.'

'And your husband has a video film or still photos of him in extremely compromising circumstances?'

Her lips framed the word 'Video' but there was no sound.

Although Samson didn't lack compassion and always had sympathy for the underdog or underbitch he also had a ruthless streak and could hound a quarry remorselessly. He hounded Maureen Hislop with, 'This man was a guest at Pinetree but had told his wife he wouldn't be home because he was working on a case?'

She couldn't speak but nodded her head.

'And you and he played bedroom games while your husband videoed the scene?'

She nodded again.

Samson knew he should now ease the pressure; protracted hostile questioning could become counter-productive and alienate the woman who had taken a risk in coming to meet him.

'Don't worry about it,' he said. 'Your secret is safe with me. And it isn't the first time I've come across the guardians of law and order indulging in naughty games. I've known at least two who use the alibi of extra duty to have extra-marital affairs. I understand and in no way condemn . . . So your husband knows my name?'

'Yes.'

'What is it?'

'Samson. Mr John Samson.'

'Does he know what I do? My job?'

'Yes. You're a private eye.'

Samson disliked this slick description of his profession, which made its members seem like paid peeping Toms but his face didn't reveal his distaste. 'Does he know the people who work for me. The names of my staff?'

She frowned. 'Your staff? I don't think so.'

'There's something else I need to know. You spoke of Colin. Did you know him by that name or as Vernon Brown?'

'I knew his true name after . . . after we became lovers.'

'Does your husband know?'

Her reply was instant. 'He does,' she said. 'But he didn't. Not for some time.' She looked around. 'I can't stay long. I might be seen.'

'You chose a public place.'

'That was no accident. Local people don't come here often. It's a tourist spot. In any other part of town I'm more likely to be seen but this is the first time I've been down here for ages.' She gave a sad smile. 'I can't afford the stuff they sell in Old Bond Street. Freddie is a tightwad. And why should I drink coffee and sample Bath buns over the way?'

She looked across the precinct in the direction of the Roman baths outside which a juggler was throwing five red balls into the air. 'I don't think I can go on with this,' she went on. 'I'd be in dead trouble if Freddie found out I'd been seen here with you.'

She made as if to rise from her seat.

'Just a minute,' said Samson quickly. 'We haven't yet talked about why you wanted to meet me, but before you tell me I'd like you to know that I think I can help you if you help me.'

131

Maureen looked puzzled. 'Help me? How?'

'I'll come to that. First, I'd like to ask you one or two things. It's clear your husband obtains blackmail material with your assistance. Whether he uses it or not doesn't matter. It's there to be used as a threat if needed. It gives him a hold. What's his hold over you? Fraudulent conversion of bank customers' money to your own account?'

She gaped at him. 'How did you know?'

'Call it an informed guess. Which bank was it?'

'You don't expect me to tell you that! It would be putting myself at your mercy. It's bad enough being at his mercy.'

Samson leaned forward. 'I do want to help you. Trust me. As for the bank, I could find out but it would take time. Which bank?'

She hesitated before saying grudgingly, 'The Capital and Provincial branch at Bristol.'

'Thank you.' He regarded her from under heavy eyelids which had sometimes given clients the impression that he was half-asleep. 'Are you afraid that if you don't obey your husband's orders he'll inform the police, and you would end up in prison?'

'I couldn't bear that,' she burst out. 'I'd sooner die!'

Samson glanced towards the next table. A man in late middle age with bushy eyebrows and a big nose was writing in a notebook. His companion was younger. She had short blonde curly hair and a wide expressive mouth; she turned her head and her eyes briefly met Samson's.

He turned to Maureen Hislop. 'Keep your voice down,' he cautioned. 'We could be overheard.'

'Sorry. I'm claustrophobic, you see. I can't travel on Tubes or go in lifts. I'd go mad in a cell.'

'Did he always use a video camera to film you with willing guests, or was it only since Colin came into your lives?'

She nodded. 'You're right. Before that I used to do what he wanted but it was just to give him kicks. I knew if I didn't he might shop me. But then Colin came along. At first everything was fine and then one day Freddie said, "Vernon takes pictures of weddings" – he was "Vernon" in those days – "wouldn't it be great if he took films of the honeymoon?" He suggested it to Colin and that's how the idea of "Video Vengeances" began. Freddie learned the video techniques and used the idea for his own ends while Colin began to advertise his services along with the adverts for kissograms, stripograms, and all the other daft things you see under the personal-services column in the local rag.'

'But they fell out?' Samson asked when she paused.

'That was because Freddie could see I was getting too fond of Colin. I wasn't supposed to do what I did for my pleasure, but for his. I told you he was cruel. He's a sadist, Mr Samson.' She looked sideways at the next table where the curly-haired woman and her escort were about to go. As they moved away, she continued, 'Not only that, but it was bad publicity for us. Colin using our address, I mean. Dumping manure on someone's lawn was the last straw. There was a terrible row and Colin was kicked out.'

'But your husband discovered that you were writing to Colin and planned to run away with him when he'd established a different sort of business with the aid of money from his wife. Am I right?'

'Yes.' Her admission was more of a helpless sigh than an affirmative.

'Was that the reason why he killed Colin?'

Her demeanour changed. 'I want him done for that,' she said viciously. 'That's why I wanted to see you today. I want him sent down for life but I know if I give evidence against him I might get something too, particularly if he rats about the money I borrowed from the bank.'

'Borrowed?'

Her voice was defiant as she replied, 'Banks can afford it. The customers didn't lose out. I expect it was written off along with all those huge debts to Third World countries.

133

Besides those debts it was nothing. A drop in the ocean.'

The table which had recently been vacated was taken over by two young women with sun-bleached hair and tanned skins. They were dressed in shirts and shorts and carried rucksacks in one hand and bottles of Coca-Cola in the other. They were talking vivaciously and volubly in French. Maureen stared at them with the disapproving look which betrays envy.

'Go on,' Samson prompted.

'I've forgotten what I was saying.'

'Tell me something else. Apart from killing Colin, your husband also killed an old woman called Daisy Simkins, didn't he?'

She looked as though the entire city of Bath had just been shaken by an earthquake. 'How did you know?'

'That doesn't matter. Why did he do it?'

'Oh, Christ!' She had gone very pale and scarcely bore any resemblance to the temptress in a dressing gown of the night before. 'He'd do the same to me if he knew what I was doing. As it is he scares me half to death.'

'Why did he kill Miss Simkins?'

She didn't answer his question directly but seemed to be following a different train of thought. 'They've got some other poor sod for Colin's murder, and they don't know who did the old girl in.'

'Why did he kill Miss Simkins?'

'If Freddie hadn't killed Colin I wouldn't be here now. That did it for me. I want him put away.'

'Quite. But why did he kill Miss Simkins? Why did he kill in cold blood an old lady who had never harmed him and lived on her own?'

'Isn't it obvious? She stood in the way.'

'Stood in the way of what?'

'Colin knew she was going to leave all her money to his wife and he stupidly told Freddie. I don't know which of them thought it up but you don't have to be a genius to work out that if the old girl could be got rid of, and if Colin

134

got friendly with his wife again, and pretended his memory had come back, he might get a slice of the grabs.'

'You didn't mind him getting friendly with his wife again?'

'I wasn't in a position to, was I? And anyway, she was a dead loss. He didn't love her. He loved me. And I didn't know anything about it until after it happened. Don't try to implicate me.'

She sounded aggressive.

'I'm not trying to implicate you,' said Samson. 'If I'm right, your husband killed Miss Simkins so that your lover could gain some money from his wife. Didn't your husband expect a cut?'

'That's exactly it. He did. That was before they fell out, before they fell out over me and the way Colin operated his video vengeances. Colin left Pinetree but he didn't let Freddie know where he was going. He told me, of course. I knew. Freddie was mad. He had no right to be. After all, he'd told Colin to clear off and then was angry because he didn't know where he'd gone.' She shook her head in mystification. 'It wasn't logical, but Freddie isn't always logical.' After a moment's reflection she went on, 'I think Freddie didn't really believe Colin would go. He thought he could control Colin like he controlled me.'

'Did your husband know Mr Coomber as "Colin" at that time or was he still "Vernon Brown"?'

'Colin told Freddie his true name but he traded as Vernon Brown and we called him "Mr Brown" in front of other people.'

'How did your husband find out where Colin had gone?' Samson asked.

She looked around before answering as though to make sure no one in the precinct was watching her.

'He caught me writing to Colin. I thought he was out in the garden trimming the edges of his blessed lawn. But he sneaked up behind me.' She winced at the memory. 'He wanted to know where Colin was. It was awful.'

'How do you mean – awful?'

135

'We've got a cellar at Pinetree. I never go in it. It hasn't got a window or anything. It's cold and dark. I hate it. It's where Freddie keeps all his photographic equipment and his cassettes. He and Colin used it to develop the vengeances films. There's a screen in there too and a TV set. Well, Freddie dragged me down there and locked me in. And he switched off the strip lighting from outside. I was in pitch dark. I nearly went mad. I've told you, I'm claustrophobic. After two hours I was on my knees begging, screaming to be let out. He made me call out Colin's address – the hotel where he was staying – before unlocking the door.'

She paused. 'And then?' Samson prompted.

'And then,' she said, 'I did what he told me. It wasn't the first time he'd put me in the cellar. He'd done it once before but only for about ten minutes. That was when I'd refused to go and chat up a guest, a nasty old man who smelled like a rubbish tip on a hot day. Being locked up is something I've always had hanging over my head.'

'What did he tell you to do?' Samson asked quietly.

'I had to ring Colin at his hotel and say it was urgent that we met, not to tell him why, but to explain when we met.'

'And did you call him?'

'Yes. He asked what it was all about, naturally. I said I couldn't speak but I'd be up on the late train that day. It would be dangerous to go to his hotel, and would he meet me outside the Friend at Hand Tavern. That was the place Freddie chose. He knows that part of London quite well and knew it was only a little way from Colin's hotel. I said I'd be there at midnight. I couldn't make it any earlier. And then I said, "I've got to go. I can hear him," and I rang off. I was shaking all over, I can tell you. Freddie was right behind me all the time.'

The French girls at the next table rose from their chairs, adjusted the rucksacks on their backs, and moved away. Their places were immediately taken by a middle-aged couple wearing peaked red caps and speaking in American

136

accents. After depositing a tray holding plates of hamburgers, coleslaw and chips, and cups of coffee, they spread a map on the table.

Movements at the adjacent table seemed to disturb Maureen Hislop. She fidgeted in her seat and said, 'I can't go on. I really can't. I shouldn't have come.' She reached down for her handbag and shopping bag and made as if to leave.

'Wait,' said Samson in a firm voice. 'You've told me far too much to stop now. What happened when you went to London on the late train? You met Colin as arranged?'

'Yes.'

'And what about your husband? Was he there with you?'

She looked very uneasy. 'Not exactly.'

'He was watching?'

'Yes.'

Samson nodded. 'I get the picture. You were the decoy.'

'I didn't know it was going to end like that,' she cried out, oblivious to the danger of being overheard. 'Honest I didn't!'

'Please keep your voice down.'

'Sorry. I didn't know it would end like that. I thought there would be an argument and maybe Colin would give in and share some of the money he'd got.'

'So while you kept Colin talking your husband stole up from behind and slit his throat.'

She shuddered. 'It was horrible,' she whispered. 'I got blood on my dress. I had to burn it when we got home.'

'Do you know where he got the knife he used, something called a *kukri*?'

'I didn't at the time but afterwards I found out it had once belonged to Colin. It had been given to him years ago, by a friend I suppose, long before the trouble with his memory. It was something he'd hung on to through thick and thin. Don't ask me why. Anyway it was what Freddie used on the old lady and he'd never given it back.' She gave Samson an anguished look. 'You don't know how

137

guilty I feel. I led Colin into a trap. I've had nightmares ever since, Mr Samson. And I'm frightened. I'm afraid the same might happen to me. He's done it twice, he might do it three times.'

'Then we shall have to make sure he doesn't,' said Samson in an effort to give reassurance but she seemed not to hear him.

'Freddie makes out I'm not very bright,' she went on, 'but I'm bright enough to know a detective from London doesn't come to stay at Pinetree twice without good reason, and the reason could be to do with Colin. I thought that and I think Freddie thinks the same. That's why I wrote you the note I did.' She looked earnestly at him. 'You said a little while ago you might be able to help me.'

'I did, and I hope I can.'

'If it means going into a witness box I don't think I could bear it, particularly if Freddie rats about the money I took from the bank. I might even be accused of murder with him.' She wrinkled her brow, 'Is it called an accessory or a conspiracy or something?'

'It might not be easy to keep you out of it altogether,' said Samson, 'but I'll do my best.'

'Are you here on account of Miss Simkins or because of Colin?'

Samson gave a slight smile. 'I don't normally disclose who I'm acting for but this case is different. I don't see why you shouldn't know. I'm here on behalf of the man who has been wrongly accused of Colin's murder.'

'Oh.'

'Did you know he was Colin's half-brother?'

'Well, I did wonder, I must admit. I knew a bit about the family history but I didn't know his half-brother's surname, and to be honest I didn't really want to know. But when I read in the papers that the chap who'd been charged was a dealer in rare old knives and suchlike it did ring a bit of a bell.'

'I think it probable that the *kukri* might have been

138

given to Colin by him many years ago, perhaps as a present at Christmas.'

'Some present!' Maureen Hislop shook her head. 'I'd be scared stiff if someone gave me a knife as a present.'

On the far side of the precinct the juggler had moved away and his place had been taken by a young man with a violin who appeared to be arguing with an official.

'What are you going to do?' asked Maureen after a pause.

'I shall be returning to Pinetree this evening and I shall ask if there's a vacancy. I shall say that business here was better than I expected. Your husband won't believe me, of course, but he'll pretend to. I might even ask if it isn't too much of an imposition if I might have the use of his room for one more night as I liked it there so much.'

'You will?' She sounded amazed.

'Yes, and I might hint that I'd welcome some female company.'

'You know what'll happen.'

'I think so, and when it does we'll take it from there.' He leaned across the table. 'It'll mean you getting into bed with me but don't be surprised if you find that I haven't undressed.'

'Aren't you afraid?' she asked wonderingly. 'Freddie may not look strong, but he is. And he prides himself on knowing a bit about martial arts.'

'I'm usually able to look after myself,' said Samson.

For the first time she smiled. It lighted her face and she looked like the woman he had first seen when visiting the guest house. 'Samson by name and Samson by nature,' she said with a laugh.

'Not Samson by nature,' he corrected. 'There is no Delilah in my life.'

'You're not married then?'

'No.'

'I'm surprised.'

'I'm not Samson by nature or Adonis by looks.'

'Does that matter? It wouldn't matter to most women.

What counts is that you seem strong and reliable. And I'll bet you're not short of a bob or two.'

'Quite right,' said Samson, 'and if ever I need a character reference I'll come to you.'

She gave another little laugh and then, 'I really must go.'

'There's just one other thing,' he said, 'and it's important.'

'What's that?'

'I assume you do the flower arrangements in the house.'

'That's right. Why?'

'I noticed there was a vase of pink carnations in the hall this morning. If you change your mind and don't want to go through with coming to my bedroom, or something has happened that really puts *your* life at risk if I stay the night, alter that flower arrangement in the hall. Make it different flowers or even nothing at all. Have you got that? It is important.'

'I've got it.' She gathered her bags and stood up. 'I shan't let you down. And I'll only change the flowers if there's some really good reason. If that happens I'll try to be here same time tomorrow to explain.' She began moving away. 'Be seeing you,' she said.

He watched her disappear behind a throng of tourists and then went in search of a pub. He had a pressing need for refreshment stronger than coffee.

14

In a narrow alleyway not far from Binks he found a pub called the Volunteer Rifleman's Arms. The small dimly lit bar was crowded, but by elbowing and nudging he was eventually served with a lager and a steak sandwich. Having temporarily satisfied thirst and hunger he went in search of a telephone.

'Georgia? Put me through to Shandy, will you . . . Shandy, cancel everything. I want you here.'

'Oh, sure. No problem except that Paul and Kimberley will need their evening meal and I had to leave home in a hurry this morning and the washing machine hasn't been emptied. On top of that I've got two appointments this afternoon and I want to slip out sometime to M and S to change a dress I bought yesterday. Oh yes, and there's some late-night shopping I need to do. Apart from those insignificant items, no problem.'

'Good. Have you got the tape running and I'll explain.'

'Go ahead.'

Samson told her what had occurred the previous evening and then gave an account of his meeting with Maureen Hislop. He went on, 'I want you to come down and book in at Pinetree Guest House. If questions are asked you can be a sales rep for a couturier and you're calling at shops in Old Bond Street as well as others in the city, or else invent something you can back up.'

'What if they have no vacancies?'

'I think they will have, but if they don't, meet me

outside the Pump Room at eight and we'll take it from there.'

'If he knows who you are and what you do he might know about me.'

'I asked Maureen if he knew the names of my staff and she said he didn't, but if it worries you book in under your maiden name.'

'And once I'm inside what then?'

'If I can manage it,' said Samson, 'I'll have the room I had last night. That might not be easy but I shall try for it. As I've said, it's on the top floor and opposite Maureen's. But whichever room I'm in I want to be caught *in flagrante delicto*.'

A long silence followed and then Shandy said, 'Have you gone mad?'

'Madness, like beauty, is in the eye of the beholder.'

'Don't get philosophical on me,' said Shandy a trifle impatiently. 'Don't push your luck. I'll come, but I want to know what I'm supposed to do once I'm there.'

Samson told her.

'Do you think it will work?' she asked.

'If it doesn't we're in for all sorts of legal actions. Conspiracy, committing offences by deception, trespass – you name it. Are you still on?'

'Of course I'm on. But I think I'll increase my life insurance cover. Hislop sounds a very nasty character indeed.'

'He is. By the way, if we should bump into each other there, we are strangers.'

'You don't need to spell it out. If we do meet by chance, so far as I'm concerned you'd simply be a overweight stranger badly in need of a restricted diet.'

After giving a few more instructions, Samson signed off.

At the other end of the line Shandy put down the handset. For a few moments she sat gazing at a vase of flowers at the end of her desk. Like the flowers in the reception hall of the guest house these were pink carnations. Samson had mentioned the signal of changed flowers but she couldn't recall everything he'd said. It would be necessary to run back the tape but before that she had another task. She pressed an intercom key.

'Georgia, can you spare a moment?'

'Sure.'

Shandy didn't waste time in explanations. When Georgia came into her room she said, 'You come into your own today. You'll be in sole charge of the office, and I shall want you to take one of my interviews. I'll leave you the file. It's pretty straightforward. A small-time tycoon wants his ex-girlfriend followed. I'll leave a list of other jobs. All being well Mr Samson and I should be back tomorrow but if anyone wants either of us urgently just stall, stall, stall. Okay?'

Georgia's eyes were shining. 'Great,' she said. 'This is something I've dreamed of. It's like' – she paused to search for an analogy – 'it's like an unseeded player reaching the final at Wimbledon.'

Shandy flicked back the wayward lock of hair from her forehead. 'Make sure you win,' she said, 'and don't drop a set.'

At exactly seven in the evening she pressed the door-bell of Pinetree Guest House. When there was no response after a reasonable time she pressed the bell again. Almost at once the door was opened by a woman who Shandy instantly realised must be Maureen Hislop.

'Good evening. I wonder if you've got a room for the night.'

Maureen looked at her closely. 'I don't think we have. Sorry.'

'There's a notice "Vacancies" on the board by your gate.'

At that moment Hislop appeared. 'Maureen is mistaken,' he said. 'We are fairly full but we do have one room left. Number five.'

Maureen protested. 'But Freddie, I thought that one was to be kept free.'

143

'We can accommodate this lady. We don't know if the gentleman will be coming back.'

'He said to me before he left that he probably would.'

Hislop ignored her. 'Have you come by car?' he asked.

'Train,' said Shandy. 'I've got an interview for a job first thing tomorrow so I thought I'd stay the night in Bath.'

'Come in,' said Hislop.

As she entered Shandy looked for and saw a vase of pink carnations. So far, so good, she thought.

'What job are you after?' asked Hislop as she signed the register.

'I'm a teacher. English language and literature. It's a school job.'

'Which school would that be, if you don't mind me asking?'

Shandy was glad she had prepared her cover before leaving London. 'Granemont Girls' Preparatory School,' she said.

'Isn't that near Tollbridge Road?'

'Yes, I believe so. Can I see my room please?'

Hislop picked up her bag. 'Let me carry this . . . Not very heavy,' he remarked as he led her upstairs. 'I hope this will suit,' he said as they entered a room. 'The loo, and bath if you want it, is over the corridor.' He deposited the bag on the floor. 'If there's anything you need, Maureen and I will be happy to oblige.'

'Thank you.'

Hislop lingered by the door. 'Teachers get younger and younger,' he said. 'You don't look old enough to be teaching.'

Shandy wished he would leave. His prolonged stare made her uneasy. 'I can assure you I am old enough,' she said briskly.

'You must be older than you look,' he went on, 'just as I'm younger than I look. Never judge by appearances is my motto. I'm a very fit man. To look at me I don't suppose you'd guess I'm skilled in the martial arts.'

Shandy made no comment but her sense of unease increased. She didn't like his fixed gaze, in which there was a sort of salacious appreciation.

'Very fit,' he continued. 'Fit as any younger man and just as capable physically, if you take my meaning. Ask Maureen.'

'If you'll excuse me,' said Shandy firmly, 'I'd like to do my unpacking.'

'I shouldn't be delaying you but we don't often get single ladies staying here on their own. I mustn't hold you up. Will you be going out for a meal?'

'I've already eaten.'

'Then you'll be staying in, I expect. Don't forget, if there's anything you want I shall be only too pleased to oblige.'

Shandy gave a curt nod of the head.

As the door closed behind him she sat down on the side of the bed. Her shoulders sagged and she let out her breath. 'Phew!'

This was going to be an assignment with Samson which she knew she would not enjoy.

When she had unpacked the few belongings she'd thrown into the bag she cautiously opened the door and peered outside. A man, carrying a briefcase, head bowed, was stumping up the stairs. She darted back into her room. When she judged the coast was clear she emerged again. This time there was nobody in sight. She went a few feet along the corridor and saw that what appeared to be a linen cupboard was next to her room. She tried the door. It was locked. Back in her room she calculated that if the mirror over the washbasin was two-way anyone in the linen cupboard could view her in bed.

She checked the time on her watch. Samson was due to try to book a room within seven minutes. She badly wanted to put through a call to her home to make sure that her husband and daughter were coping. When she'd tried to ring earlier the line had been engaged. She'd noticed a pay-phone in the reception area below but she didn't want to risk being overheard. With each passing minute the assignment became more unpleasant; it was only the loyalty she felt for Samson which kept her from dashing to the station to catch the next train back to London.

At seven-thirty exactly she opened her door again. She could hear voices below and although she couldn't distinguish the spoken words she recognised one of the voices as Samson's.

After making the call to Shandy, Samson had driven to Bristol. At the Capital and Provincial Bank he used a ploy which never failed. He presented his professional card and asked to see the bank manager as a matter of urgency. To the manager he explained that he had been instructed by a firm of solicitors to find the whereabouts of one Frederick Hislop, who if traced might learn something greatly to his advantage. It was understood that Mr Hislop had once worked at the bank.

'I'm new here,' the manager had said, 'and so are most of the staff. There's been a reorganisation but we do have one member of staff who might know about Mr Hislop. Failing that, I daresay head office would be able to provide you with his last-known address. But first we'll see if Mr Pearson can help you.'

The manager took Samson into a small private room which adjoined his office. Samson placed his recording briefcase with its concealed microphone on a table and sat down. Within two minutes an elderly clerk appeared who introduced himself as Mr Pearson. A recurrent tic near his left eye made it seem that he was winking at Samson.

'I remember Freddie Hislop,' he said, 'but I don't know where he is now. No idea at all. He married one of our cashiers. Someone called Maureen Gengist. Both gave in their notices.' Winking furiously he added, 'Maureen did send us a postcard while she was on honeymoon in the

146

Costa Brava, but after that we didn't hear from either of them again.'

'What was he like?' Samson asked.

'What was he like? He was a conscientious sort. He would work late. But so would Maureen. That's how it all started, I think. It surprised us when they got hitched. He was a bit of a loner and she was an extravert, and a bit of a flirt too. That might have been her French connection.'

'French connection?' Samson enquired.

'Her father was French. From over the pond. Calais, if I remember rightly. He married a Bristol woman and I believe he became naturalised British. I know Maureen had relations in Calais. She used to have holidays there. That is, until Freddie Hislop came along.' Pearson looked reflective as, with a series of tics, he added, 'I expect you know he was a divorced man.'

'I had heard that,' Samson lied. 'Do you recall the name of his first wife?'

'No. We didn't know too much about him. He played the cards close to his chest.' The habitual and involuntary spasm by his left eye made it seem that Pearson was hinting at some dark ambiguity by referring to cards close to the chest.

'Do you know why he was divorced?' Samson asked.

'That's a difficult one to answer. Nobody knew.'

'And you've no idea where they might have gone?'

'None at all, sir. But, between you and me, I couldn't see it lasting. Maureen was flighty, if you take my meaning. I can't see someone like Freddie Hislop putting up with that. I think he would have soon put her in order. He was a physical-fitness freak and, in his way, I'd think he was quite a hard man. In fact, it was rumoured that this side of his nature had led to his first wife divorcing him.'

When he left the bank Samson knew he had learned very little but at least the visit had occupied part of the afternoon. He returned to Bath and spent the rest of the afternoon like any sightseer or tourist admiring the Palladian architecture of the Royal Crescent and taking tea in the Pump Room.

On his return to the guest house he was met by Hislop, who was mowing the front lawn.

'Back again, Mr Dan.'

'Back again.'

'I trust you had a satisfactory day,' said Hislop, switching off the mower.

'Most satisfactory.'

'You want to stay another night in our lovely city. More business?'

'Some more.'

'And you'd like to stay here at Pinetree?'

'I would.'

Hislop shook his head. 'I hope I shan't disappoint you but I've got an idea that we're full tonight, but come with me.'

They went to the reception hall and Hislop began thumbing through the register. 'I'm afraid it does look as though we're full up tonight, Mr Dan.' He gave a quick look as if to gauge Samson's reaction to this news. And then, 'If you'd phoned through a booking we could have saved a room but a young lady has taken the last available one.'

No flicker of disappointment passed over Samson's impassive features but inwardly he was concerned about the dilemma which would face Shandy if he was unable to stay.

'What a pity,' he said, 'I shall have to look elsewhere. A great pity. It's not everywhere one can find such comforts as you offer here.' He heaved a sigh. 'Companionship for the lonely is so necessary sometimes.'

Hislop's eyes narrowed so much that he was squinting as he peered closely at Samson. 'I thought you were the sort of man who didn't need a close companionship.'

'Usually I don't, but tonight I should welcome it.'

Hislop picked up a pencil and let it play a light tattoo on the table-top. He seemed to be weighing up a problem. Eventually he put down the pencil and said, 'I'm not sure I know what you want. Maureen is better at relationships.

I've never been all that good on that score. But she's a sensitive woman and won't push herself when her company isn't wanted.'

'I envy you having the comfort of a woman like that.'

Hislop picked up the pencil and began tapping it on the table again. 'You put me in an awkward position, Mr Dan. I don't really want to spend another night downstairs.' The word 'fruitless' had hovered unspoken over the last part of the sentence.

'I'm willing to pay over the odds for accommodation. I like it here and don't want to have to go searching for another place.'

Hislop put down the pencil. 'Over the odds, eh? You're tempting me, Mr Dan. My room would cost quite a bit more tonight. Eighty pounds at least.'

Samson considered the proposition. 'All right,' he said at length, 'make it eighty. And I'd like it if you or your wife would bring me a whisky at eleven o'clock. It's my regular nightcap.'

'With water?'

'Mineral water please.'

'At eleven prompt?'

'At eleven.'

'That can be arranged but let's be specific. Who do you want to bring the drink? Maureen or me?'

'If Maureen would be willing . . . ' Samson left the sentence unfinished.

Hislop gave a thin smile. 'She'll be willing. I want to turn in early tonight myself. I shall be out of the way.' He gave a meaningful look.

'Good. I'm going out for a meal now but I'll be back by ten-thirty.'

Samson understood and approved the custom of allowing a condemned man to choose the menu for his last meal on earth. It was a privilege masquerading as a small mercy after judicial clemency had been merciless. It was the decent thing to do, and in a business context was the equivalent of an employer saying to a dismissed employee, 'I'm sorry to have to sack you but have a drink on me before you go.'

Even the Puritan ethic of 'We eat to live; we don't live to eat' was abandoned in the face of eternal darkness. To Samson it seemed a black irony that food, which sustains life, should be offered so generously to someone about to die.

With this attitude in mind he went once more to Popjoy's Restaurant. He, self-condemned to go to bed with the wife of a man he was sure was both a murderer and a blackmailer, needed the fortification of an excellent meal. It might, or might not, be his last, but he was determined to make the most of it.

As a starter he selected wild-boar and guinea-fowl terrine with an apricot and ginger marmalade. For the entrée he had saddle of roe deer with a pear gratin and green and pink peppercorn sauce and he completed the condemned man's meal with Alpine strawberry sorbet with a slice of fresh mango. Choice of wine to accompany the meal wasn't easy but he settled for claret and a ten-year-old bottle of Château-Lafite. As a final self-indulgence he went for coffee and Cointreau to an upstairs lounge where, it was reputed, the ghost of Juliana Popjoy, Beau Nash's mistress, might sometimes wander. Disappointingly it was one of her nights off.

He returned to Pinetree Guest House a couple of minutes before his stated time of ten-thirty. Hislop, who must have been listening for any arrivals, came out of a back room.

'I see you're back, Mr Dan. You had a good meal, I trust.'

'Your trust isn't misplaced,' replied Samson.

'I'm off duty now. I've told Maureen to bring you your whisky at eleven. We do our best – Maureen does her best – to please.'

'Passing ships, Mr Hislop?'

'Passing ships, Mr Dan.'

'Good night,' said Samson as he made his way towards the stairs.

150

15

Ability to cope with the unexpected is essential in any trade or profession involving personal danger. Samson's ability was put on test when, on entering the bedroom, he saw that a bottle of whisky and a bottle of mineral water had been placed, with a glass, on a bedside table.

Shandy's instructions had been to wait and watch for Maureen Hislop bringing up the whisky at around eleven o'clock. This was to be the signal for her first to check that Hislop wasn't in the private quarters and then to go to the cellar and unlock its door with a key gun. Then, while Samson was engaged in playing a scene with Maureen for the benefit of her watching husband, Shandy would remove some of the video cassettes and search for anything which might incriminate Hislop as either blackmailer or murderer.

He was wondering whether he had miscalculated, and whether Hislop wasn't intending to play voyeur that night, when there was a tap on the door and Maureen entered. She was wearing a low-cut white blouse and a short tight-fitting black leather skirt. Her shoes were black with ankle-straps and had stiletto heels. In her arms she carried bed sheets and before she spoke her eyes flicked towards the two-way mirror.

'I've come to change the sheets, Mr Dan,' she said. 'I'm sorry, I should have done it earlier.'

From the signal with her eyes it was evident that Hislop was in position and watching, and probably video-taping the bedroom scene.

'Why do you need to change the sheets?' Samson asked.

'After you left this morning I stripped the bed and put Freddie's sheets back on,' she replied. 'He likes sheets. I prefer a duvet myself.' She began unmaking the bed and Samson realised that she was following a scenario devised by her husband. She moved with a sinuous grace which made her ordinary task seem like an invitation to sensual imaginings.

But her performance was mostly lost on Samson, who was disconcertingly aware that it wasn't yet twenty minutes to eleven. Would Shandy know the whisky was already in place or would she be waiting for Maureen Hislop to appear with it at around eleven o'clock? And would she know that Hislop had gone straight to his viewing closet after he, Samson, had gone upstairs? He didn't know which room Shandy was occupying but he knew she must be in the house not only because of Hislop's remark that a young woman had booked in but because as a fail-safe Samson had instructed her to leave a mark on the gate-post if she'd been unable to obtain accommodation. There had been no mark. He was now left with the prospect of playing a seduction scene without knowing how long it could safely be prolonged to give Shandy time, if she was aware of what had happened, to collect any evidence from the cellar.

The sheets had been pulled off and Maureen paused in her work to say, 'I like duvets. You don't have to go through this stripping business so often. Not that I mind stripping,' she added, giving a flirtatious look as though to underline a naughty ambiguity.

It was a great effort, but Samson managed to play along with the *double entendre* by saying, 'I like women who can strip. Strip beds, I mean.'

He tried to appear relaxed but his mind was working in overdrive. Hislop knew he was a private investigator and might even have suspected that Shandy was a planted ally. Although this seemed unlikely, it was a possibility which couldn't be discounted. Hislop had been clever enough to

152

throw the time schedule out of gear by having the whisky already provided and sending Maureen to change the sheets well ahead of eleven o'clock. It had been a mistake to have made such an insistent point about times.

The prospect of having to appear to encourage Maureen while at the same time having to resist any too intimate advances by her appalled him. And yet, unless he could maintain a convincing delaying tactic, Shandy would have no opportunity to visit the cellar if, indeed, she knew it was safe to do so.

Maureen was laying the bed sheets as though they were symbols of some arcane religio-sexual ritual. The humdrum job of bed-making had never before struck Samson as erotically stimulating but Maureen with her manual smoothing of creases and tempting looks directed at him was making the lower sheet look like an unwritten invitation to an anything-goes party.

'What about the other sort of woman?' she asked.

'What other sort?'

'The sort that doesn't just strip beds but strips herself.'

She seemed to be enjoying the situation and Samson wondered if she was still on his side, wishing to pin down and convict the murderer of her lover, or whether since their meeting she had changed her mind and was now collaborating with her husband.

'It's only natural, isn't it?' she asked, and paused from bed-making.

Samson felt as though he was walking blind on crutches through a minefield saturated with explosives. 'Natural?' he asked with an unnaturally dry mouth.

'It's only natural to like women who are willing to strip,' she said.

'Very natural.'

'Men have their needs and so do women. Some men don't understand that we women have needs just as strong as theirs.'

'I'm sure that is so.'

She changed the pillow-slip and then hugged the pillow to her in an embrace. 'Do you have natural needs, Mr Dan?'

'Sometimes,' said Samson, the word half-choking him.

'Are you married?' she asked.

It was a question to which she already knew the answer. Why had she asked it? Had it been scripted by Hislop? He was glad she was on the other side of the bed. So long as she stayed there he could stall for time, but it was difficult to stall indefinitely.

'I've never felt the need for marriage,' he said.

She gave a coy look and then took him completely by surprise by throwing the pillow at him. 'Catch!'

Samson grabbed the pillow.

She laughed and unbuttoned the front of her blouse which she pulled open to expose her breasts.

'I've never felt a need for marriage either,' she said, 'but I am married. But I don't let that get in the way of my pleasure. Luckily I've got a very understanding husband.'

She started to move slowly round the bed like a feline predator stalking a mouse. Samson clasped the pillow as though it was protective armour.

'Put it down,' she said. 'You look daft holding it like that.'

Samson held the pillow even tighter.

She advanced a couple of paces, closing in on him. 'Does it put you off that I'm married?' she asked and without waiting for a reply went on, 'A lot of men find it more exciting with a married woman. All right, so it's adultery. But adultery can be a big thrill if you've got the nerve. Are you a man with nerve?'

He was aware that she had positioned herself so that anyone peering through the mirror would have a perfect view of them facing each other beside a bed.

'It's not a question of nerve,' he said. 'I've got a difficulty.'

'A what?'

'A difficulty.'

'Don't worry about that. Maureen knows how to rouse sleeping dogs.'

'It's not that sort of difficulty.'

She looked perplexed. 'What's the difficulty then? Don't you fancy me?'

'It's not that.'

'Glad to hear it,' she said pertly.

'It's psychological.'

She advanced towards him and reached for the pillow. 'Let me have that.' He allowed her to take the pillow, which she dropped on the bed. 'Now tell Maureen what your psychological difficulty is.' She sat on the side of the half-made bed and patted the place beside her. 'Come and sit down and tell Maureen your problem. She's good at sorting out men's problems for them.'

Her use of the third person singular coincided with a change in the image she had previously projected. It was as if a separate and different personality had taken over from the one she had manifested at the restaurant. Her voice was the same, her face was the same, but Samson had the uncanny feeling that he was in the presence of a total stranger, someone who was unrelated to the earlier Maureen Hislop. When she had first come into the bedroom he had thought she was acting a part; now she was no longer acting, she was living the part.

'Come on,' she crooned, 'don't be a silly boy. Sit down and tell Maureen what's worrying you.'

'It's not easy,' he said.

'Tell Maureen,' she soothed, and she pulled the blouse off her right shoulder as if preparing to offer the milk of human kindness or any other form of nourishment.

'It's to do with cleanliness,' he said.

'Are you saying I'm not clean?' she demanded, seductiveness changing to annoyance.

'It's not you, it's me.'

She frowned. 'You haven't got it, have you?'

'Got what?'

155

'AIDS.'

'No.'

'VD?'

He shook his head. 'No.' Sensing he had gained the initiative he played a little longer for time. 'I have to be clean,' he said. 'It's a compulsion. I can't go to bed with anyone unless I've just showered and cleaned my teeth. I'm very keen on bodily and oral hygiene. It's almost an obsession. You came up here too soon. I wasn't expecting you until eleven. I'd have had the opportunity to shower by then.'

She gave a quick glance in the direction of the mirror as though seeking assistance from an invisible controller. To anyone unaware that they were being watched the brief glance would have meant nothing, but to Samson it was confirmation that Hislop was in position. He hoped fervently that Shandy was exploring the cellar.

'All right,' she said. 'You go and have your shower, but don't be long. Maureen doesn't like to be kept waiting. She wants to give you comfort and she's very good at that.'

'I'm sure she is,' replied Samson, moving fleet-footed towards the *en suite* bathroom.

As he was closing the door she called out again, 'Don't be long.'

Once inside the bathroom Samson locked the door and turned on the shower. But he didn't undress. Instead, he put down the lid of the WC and sat on it.

Ten minutes passed.

Maureen Hislop knocked on the door. 'Hurry up!'

The shower was still running. Samson turned it off.

'Hurry up,' she called again.

'Shan't be long,' he called back, resuming his seat.

Another five minutes passed. Another knock on the door.

'What are you doing in there?'

'Cleaning my teeth,' Samson called back in a muffled voice. 'Oral hygiene. Very important.'

He heard her say something which sounded like 'Christ!'

Three minutes later he emerged from the bathroom.

She was lying on her back on the bed naked except for tiny black panties. 'You took long enough,' she accused.

'Sorry about that.'

'And why are you still dressed? You didn't have to dress again.'

'It's all part of my problem,' said Samson.

This time there was no mistaking what she said.'Christ! You're a funny one, and that's a fact.'

'Can't help it,' he said.

'What is it now then?'

'The light.'

'The light!'

'I don't like being seen without my clothes on. That's why I got dressed after my shower. And I can't undress again while the light is on.'

'Are you mucking me about?' she asked suspiciously.

'No. It's the truth. I've even been under analysis for the condition. It was a failure. The analyst said I must have had a deep trauma as a baby one day while my nappy was being changed. I hadn't wanted my private parts exposed. He might have been right but it didn't help in the least. That didn't stop him charging a small fortune for his services.'

'You mean you've never done it with the light on?' she asked incredulously.

'Never. Not once.'

'Then it's time you learned.' She gave an encouraging smile. 'Forget about that silly analyst. Maureen will teach you. She's a good teacher, better than any analyst.'

'I'm sure she is, but the pupil is unwilling.'

'You seriously want the lights off?'

'Yes.'

'Well, I don't. Anyway, they say it's working class to do it in the dark. You working class?'

'I'm very working class. My mother was a scullery maid and my father a street sweeper.'

During this exchange Maureen Hislop had raised herself

157

and was now lying on her side. With arm crooked she was supporting her chin with her hand. 'I've never met anyone like you,' she said. 'No, I tell a lie. There was a schoolboy once. He was terribly shy. Are you shy?'

'I suppose I must be.'

She thought for a moment. 'Tell you what,' she said, 'I'll switch off the light so you can get undressed and into bed in the dark. Then we'll have it on again. I don't like the dark. You wouldn't know this, but the light is always on in my bedroom, all night long.'

Samson sensed she was telling the truth. If so, to have been locked in an unlighted cellar must have intensified her claustrophobia.

'You switch off the overhead light,' she said, 'and I'll switch off the bedside lights.'

'Right.' Samson moved to the door and flicked off a switch on the wall.

'Now get undressed,' she said. 'See you in five minutes.'

She switched off the bed lights and the room was in darkness.

After a few seconds she said, 'I can't hear anything. You still there?'

'Yes. I'm here.'

'Don't run away.'

'I won't.'

Samson knew his delaying tactics were almost exhausted. Very gently he eased the door handle but before opening the door he said, 'I want you to close your eyes while I get into bed.'

'Whatever for? I can't see as it is.'

'Close your eyes.'

'This is stupid.'

'Close your eyes.'

'Oh, all right. They're closed.'

Samson opened the door and slipped outside. He was counting on her having her eyes closed and not seeing the illumination from the landing light as the door was opened. She made no sound. He closed the door quietly and moved to the nearby door which gave access to the viewing closet.

'Come out, Hislop,' he said loudly.

16

The door swung open and Hislop leaped out, knife in hand, and slashed at Samson's throat. Samson parried the blow with his right arm. The knife slit his coat sleeve and gashed his forearm. Blood welled out of a deep cut. Momentarily off balance he wasn't able to recover in time to stop another attack. The knife descended in a glittering arc but he managed to sway to one side and the knife sliced through the shoulder padding of his coat and did little more than scratch his shoulder.

Hislop continued the frenzied attack with a scything movement which, had it connected, might have disembowelled the fat detective, but Samson with speed born of a strong survival instinct and experience in rough-house brawls grabbed Hislop's striking wrist, held it like a vice, and then threw himself on to the carpeted landing floor. As he fell he twisted Hislop's wrist. The fall and the sudden twist made Hislop give a scream of pain as, unable to maintain his balance, he fell beside Samson. As he fell a sound like a pistol shot came from his wrist.

Samson stood up while Hislop writhed on the floor gripping a broken wrist with his other hand. The knife had spun away and was lying halfway down the stairs.

Maureen Hislop appeared in the bedroom doorway. Her face was torn with shock. Samson knew at once that her dissociated personality had vanished and she was once again the frightened woman he had met at the restaurant.

She looked at her agonised husband on the floor and at

the blood staining the sleeve of Samson's coat. Her mouth opened as though she was going to speak but no sound emerged.

Samson smiled and said, 'Just as well I didn't get undressed. This coat has taken a lot of punishment. I must remember to send in a bill for damage done.'

A man wearing pyjamas appeared at the foot of the stairs. 'What's going on up there?' he called peevishly. 'Some of us need to get to sleep.'

'Go back to bed,' said Samson. 'You won't be disturbed again, I promise.'

Muttering something about bloody inconsiderate people the man retired to his room.

'Get up,' said Samson to the prone figure of Hislop.

'You've broken my wrist!'

'You're lucky I didn't break your neck. Get up.'

Hislop struggled to his feet.

'Down the stairs,' Samson ordered.

'What do you want?' Hislop groaned.

'I want quiet from you. Any noise and I'll break the other wrist.'

Samson turned to Maureen. 'You stay here and if any of the guests ask what's going on tell them your husband injured himself while trying to frame a picture but is all right now. Okay?'

She nodded her head.

'I'll be back,' said Samson, and, to Hislop, 'Get going and remember, I want quiet.'

When they reached the ground floor Samson asked, 'Where's the entrance to the cellar? In the kitchen?'

'I'll sue you for this.'

Samson gripped Hislop's arm and squeezed. 'Where's the entrance to the cellar?'

'It's in the kitchen. Get me to a hospital. I need treatment.'

'Shut up. I need treatment too.'

They passed through a living room where the TV set had

been left on and was showing the highlights of a football match. Samson paused briefly. 'I'm sorry to have missed that,' he said.

In the kitchen Hislop indicated a door. 'In there. What's all this about? There's nothing there except photographic equipment. I'm an amateur photographer. What do you want?'

Samson paused before opening the door. 'I believe the lighting switch is outside. Yes, here it is. It's on. Is somebody down there, I wonder?' He flung open the door and called out, 'Shandy!'

She emerged from behind a cabinet. 'I heard footsteps,' she said. 'I hoped it would be you but I wasn't sure.'

'I demand to be taken to hospital,' cried Hislop. 'I need treatment urgently. Get me to Casualty.'

'All in good time,' said Samson and, looking down at Shandy, 'Find anything?'

She reached for a plastic bag. 'I've taken some tapes. There are interesting titles on the covers but the most interesting is one marked "A Slice of Death". It's the only one which sounds like a murder mystery. All the others sound like porn with titles like "Sucker's Paradise" and "The Tit Worshipper". The titles are all handwritten and the porno ones are numbered but there's no number against "A Slice of Death".'

'Interesting indeed,' said Samson. 'I'd like to view "A Slice of Death".'

Hislop tried to wrest himself free from Samson's grip and almost succeeded but gave up the attempt when Samson stamped hard on the instep of his right foot. He let out a gasp of pain.

'You bastard! Are you trying to break my ankle too?'

'Any more aggravation from you and I'll do just that.'

Shandy, who had been staring at Samson's bloodied sleeve, asked, 'What's happened to you?'

'You might call it a slice of flesh. Set up the video. I want to see "A Slice of Death".'

'Not until I've had a look at your arm.'

Samson gave his prisoner a shove. 'Get going. Down.'

They went down the cellar stairs. At the bottom Samson ordered the other man to the far side of the cellar. 'Face the wall and don't move,' he said, 'unless you want more broken bones.'

Hislop obeyed.

'Take off your coat,' said Shandy. 'I'm going up to my room to get things to bind the wound. You're lucky an artery wasn't severed, but it's bad enough as it is.'

She hurried off up the stairs. When she had gone Hislop spoke. 'I've got money. I'll give you ten thousand and we'll forget all this.'

'No deal.'

'Twenty thousand.'

'Forget it,' said Samson contemptuously.

'How much then?' Hislop sounded desperate.

'All I want from you is a written and signed confession that you murdered Miss Simkins and Mr Colin Coomber.'

'I didn't. I swear I didn't.'

'Don't annoy me with stupid denials.'

'You can't prove anything.'

'I shall.'

'Has that bitch been talking to you?'

'Are you referring to your lady wife?'

'She won't go into court. She'd be terrified. Anyway, you can't compel a wife to give evidence against her husband. What's more, she knows I could do some talking which would put her behind bars.' He paused. 'You haven't got a hope of pinning anything on me. As for a written confession, how the hell do you think I could write one with a broken wrist?'

'Ah,' said Samson, 'you do have a point there. We shall have to tape a verbal confession.'

'I've got nothing to confess.'

'You killed the old lady because you were told her wealth would go to Coomber's wife, and you had learned by this time that Vernon Brown and Colin Coomber were one and the same. I don't know how much encouragement you got from Coomber to commit this crime but I believe he told you that if Miss Simkins should die you would get some of the inheritance he planned to con from his wife. How much were you to be paid?'

'I didn't do it.'

'But you and he fell out over your wife and the way he was operating "Video Vengeances". You liked the idea of vengeances involving pornographic or salacious videos but you didn't like bad publicity from manure dumping on people's lawns. Incidentally, why are you so obsessed with your lawn?'

'None of your business.'

'You were a divorced man when you married Maureen.'

'How the hell did you know that? Did that bitch tell you?'

'No. I found out for myself. I've found out a lot for myself, more than you would care for. Was the lawn obsession connected with your first marriage?'

'None of your business.'

'No, that'll be something for the prison psychiatrist to sort out. You and he can have long conversations. It'll break the dreary routine of a very long jail sentence.'

Hislop, who had been facing the wall, turned and gave a venomous glare.

'I didn't give permission to turn round. Face the wall!' As he spoke Samson took a menacing step forward. Hislop quickly turned and presented his back once more to Samson.

'Coomber gave you the knife with which you killed Miss Simkins and then you used it to kill him before you threw it away. Did you know where Coomber had got the knife in the first place?'

'I'm not saying anything.'

'Almost certainly from his half-brother, the man at present accused of his murder.'

Hislop was silent.

'Perhaps you were hoping that the knife would be traced

to the half-brother and he would take the rap for something you'd done.'

A sound from the kitchen was followed by Shandy's reappearance. She was carrying a bowl of water and a packet of tissues.

For the next two minutes she cleaned the wound on Samson's forearm and then to his surprise she said, 'Hope you don't mind.' She kicked off her shoes, lifted her skirt and peeled off her nylon tights.

'What are you doing?'

'You'll see.'

Using the remainder of the tissues as a wad against the wound she bandaged it with the tights. 'That should hold,' she said, tying a knot.

'Great. Now set up the video and we'll watch "A Slice of Death".'

Shandy was moving towards the video recorder when Hislop turned and made a dash for the stairs. She put out a bare leg, caught him on the ankle and almost tripped him. He staggered slightly and before he could recover Samson had grabbed him and put him into a fierce arm lock.

'For God's sake! You'll break my arm!'

'I might do just that. Shandy, can you look around for some rope, something to restrain this fool. Then we can watch the film in peace.'

She put down the cassette and went up the stairs. Within a minute she returned with a length of rope. 'Part of a washing line,' she said.

'It'll do.'

There were two collapsible chairs with metal frames and canvas backing in the cellar. Hislop was soon securely tied to one of these.

Shandy peered at the broken wrist, which had begun to swell. 'We'd better take that ring off his finger,' she said to Samson, 'otherwise it'll have to be cut off. The finger is puffy already.'

'You're the nurse.'

Hislop squealed as the ring was tugged from his finger.

Samson settled himself in the other chair. It was a tight fit. 'Right. Now the show can begin.'

Shandy turned on the TV receiver and adjusted it to the video channel, loaded the cassette and pressed the button marked 'Play'. Then she went and stood behind Samson, one hand resting on his shoulder.

Hislop, who had been struggling to free himself, sank back in the chair. He looked and sounded defeated as he said, 'All right. I'll come clean. Stop it!'

Samson took no notice of the plea. He stared at a flickering screen with the inscrutability of someone watching a TV commercial of an unneeded commodity.

The flickering stopped and they were watching a scene showing a wrought-iron gate set in the centre of a high macrocarpa hedge. The hand-held video camera moved in towards the gate and the next shot showed a detached house, brick built and with red-tiled roof, which looked as though it might have been constructed in the 1930s. A paved terrace ran along the front of the house and a grass lawn stretched from the terrace to the hedge. In the centre of the lawn was a circular bed filled with roses in full bloom.

'Stop it!' cried Hislop.

Again his appeal went unanswered.

The next scene was slightly out of focus. It showed an elderly woman on a bicycle which had a basket fixed to its handlebars. She was riding down a tree-lined lane. A car passed close to her and the bike wobbled. A brief shot of a dog urinating against one of the trees was followed by a closer view of the detached house. The drooping foliage of a weeping willow provided a natural frame to the picture.

'Quite artistic,' remarked Samson.

Next came a shot of the elderly woman watering the rose bed in the centre of the lawn. A telescopic lens brought the scene into close-up. The woman was small and frail, and with her bent back looked as though she was

166

afflicted with osteoporosis. Below a thin covering of wispy white hair was a brown, deeply lined face.

'This isn't your usual style, Hislop, is it?' asked Samson. 'No porno stuff here,' he added as the scene changed to one showing an open downstairs window of the house. 'Have you added estate agency to your money-making activities?' he enquired. 'Was the house up for sale?'

'It was a house I was thinking of buying to convert into a guest house. There's nothing else on the film.'

The next shot showed the house from one side. The following scene was of a greenhouse within which it was just possible to discern the old woman moving between tall plants. Another picture of the house, almost identical to the first, appeared on the screen.

'There's nothing much else,' said Hislop. 'You're wasting your time.'

'Why is the cassette sleeve marked "A Slice of Death" then?'

'I must have mixed up two cassettes; put them in the wrong covers.'

'Why did you beg me to stop the film then?'

'I thought it was something else. A cassette I bought from a man in a pub.'

The scene changed to show an old Vauxhall Viva parked near the front gate of the house. After a few seconds a man in clerical grey wearing a parson's dog-collar came through the gate and climbed into the car, which he drove away.

A momentary break in the film was followed by what looked like the interior of a sitting room. The camera panned unsteadily past an armchair and focused on an inglenook fireplace which had a row of copper pans lining its hearth. This shot dissolved into a picture of the old woman lying in bed, her throat cut, blood staining white linen.

Shandy gave a shocked gasp and turned her head away. Samson leaped to his feet and switched off the recorder. 'That'll be enough,' he said grimly.

'I didn't do it,' whined Hislop. 'It was someone else. I bought the cassette from him.'

'Tell that to the judge and jury,' retorted Samson.

A sound from the top of the stairs made him look up. Maureen Hislop, dressed once more in blouse and skirt, was staring down. Her fists were clenched and her face expressed utter disgust.

Samson, who was freeing Hislop from the chair, asked, 'Did you see it?'

'Everything. He's a monster!'

Hislop stood up, arms still tied behind his back. 'Bitch!' he snarled.

Samson gripped his arm. 'Enough of that . . . Where's the nearest police station, Maureen?'

She told him and gave directions on how to get to it.

'Move,' said Samson, giving Hislop a shove. 'Shandy, get that cassette, will you? And I'll need you to drive us but then you can come straight back here and see that Maureen is all right. I'll hand him over and wait until he's been charged.'

Hislop began mounting the stairs. When he reached his wife he said, 'You set me up. I'll get you for this,' and he spat at her.

She ducked to one side and a spasm of fear crossed her face. Then, summoning up her courage, she replied, 'You do your worst. I'll see you sent down. No wonder your first wife divorced you!'

Hislop got as far as saying, 'What about you and . . .' when Samson gripped his wrist and he broke off in a scream of pain.

'Move,' said Samson. 'Do as you're told.'

'He made me do it!' cried Maureen.

Hislop, now halfway through the kitchen, called back, 'You enjoyed it!'

Samson turned to Shandy. He was about to say something but stopped. Instead, he steered Hislop to the front door.

She was never to know that, witnessing the hatred between Hislop and his wife, he had been about to make the caustic observation that if marriages weren't made in heaven they certainly made hell on earth when he remembered her marital happiness and that she had sacrificed a night with her husband to come to his aid.

17

Returning to the guest house shortly before three in the morning Samson let himself in and found Shandy and Maureen seated at a table in the kitchen. It was evident that they had been drinking tea and eating sandwiches.

'What's the news?' asked Maureen, rising to her feet.

'He's in hospital. The idiot tried to make a run for it at the police station. He ran into the path of a car but luckily the driver managed to brake and all he's got, to add to his wrist, is fractured ribs.'

'Have the police seen the cassette?' Shandy asked.

Maureen spoke simultaneously. 'Can I get you a cup of tea or something stronger?'

'A whisky would be acceptable.'

'Please sit down. Help yourself to sandwiches. I can make some more.'

While she busied about the kitchen Samson explained the sequence of events. He and Hislop had been interviewed, after some delay, by a sergeant in a side room. It had been when Samson handed over the cassette that Hislop had rushed to the door, opened it with his good hand and bolted from the station. He had been pursued by the desk officer, who had witnessed the car accident. An ambulance had been summoned and Hislop taken to hospital. A CID sergeant had been telephoned for assistance in the enquiry and Samson had made a long statement about the murders of both Daisy Simkins and Colin Coomber. With regard to

Coomber he had been promised that the Metropolitan Police would be contacted.

'What now?' Maureen asked, putting a plate of salmon and cucumber sandwiches in front of Samson.

'It will be complicated,' he replied, reaching for a sandwich. 'The evidence against him in the case of Miss Simkins is very damaging. I think he will undoubtedly be charged with murder. It could be different with Colin.'

Maureen sat down. Her face seemed to have thinned with stress and, because she hadn't removed heavily applied cosmetics, her eye-liner and eye-shadow gave a panda-like appearance to sunken eyes. 'What do you mean,' she asked nervously.

'He'll probably deny killing Colin. Apart from you, Maureen, there are no witnesses. The police already have an accused man in custody. He is a bird in the hand. Circumstantial evidence against him is very strong. If your husband denies ever having travelled to London and there is nobody to refute it, except you, the police might not be inclined to charge him. How did you travel to London that night?'

'By car.'

'Did you stop at a garage for petrol or anything?'

'No.'

'Can you recall anyone who might be able to testify having seen you?'

She shook her head. 'No.'

'He drove there and back on one tankful of petrol?'

'Yes. We didn't stop anywhere except on the way back when he pulled in on the hard shoulder near some bushes to relieve the wants of nature. I realise now he was being deliberately careful that we shouldn't be recognised by anyone.'

Samson helped himself to another sandwich. 'These are good.'

'What does it all mean, Mr Samson?'

'I'm afraid, Maureen, it means that your evidence will be vital.'

171

'He'll try to screw me,' she burst out. 'He'll say I'm lying. It's my word against his. And he'll tell them about the money I borrowed from the bank!'

Her outburst was followed by a taut silence broken only by the faint sound of mastication and the far-off hoot of an owl.

'I couldn't bear it,' Maureen continued. 'I couldn't bear to be shut up in prison. I'd go mad!'

Shandy reached across the table and took her hand. 'You must be brave,' she said. 'You don't want Colin's death to go unpunished, do you?'

'Of course I don't.' Maureen Hislop began to sob. She said, 'Sorry,' rose from the table and pulled off a piece of kitchen towelling from a roller on the wall. Dabbing her eyes with the towelling she said between sobs, 'I can't help it. It's been too much.' She looked imploringly at the other two, her face now grotesquely streaked with smeared make-up.

'You wouldn't have an innocent man pay the penalty for a murder he didn't commit, would you?' Samson asked.

'I wouldn't want it. Naturally. But I couldn't face going into court and having to split on Freddie. He'd be staring at me with that look of his which frightens me. And then I'd be accused of robbing a bank.' She slumped down in her chair and appealed to Samson. 'What good would it do? He'd get off and I'd get two years, maybe more.'

'My client is innocent,' said Samson.

'I know that. Don't keep saying it!' She began crying again.

'We'll stand by you,' said Shandy softly. 'I expect Mr Samson will be called to give evidence. He'll tell the judge and jury how you helped him because you wanted justice done for Colin's murder.'

'That's right,' Samson agreed. 'As for the bank money, if you sell this place I don't doubt you could make a suitable reimbursement. If so, I'd guess that for repaying the money,

172

and your help in the murder trial, you'd only get a suspended sentence.'

In spite of her distress Maureen managed to say, 'You're twisting my arm.'

'Perhaps. But I don't want an innocent man sent down. And I'd speak up for you and say that, but for you, another murder could have remained unsolved.'

Shandy squeezed Maureen's hand. 'Be strong,' she said.

Maureen pulled her hand away. 'It's all very well for you to tell me to be strong but it's not happening to you.' She shook her head. 'In a way, I hated Freddie, but I relied on him. I've never been very good on my own. Never have been. All right. He dominated me and made me do things. But I depended on him. Now he's gone and I don't know what to do.'

Samson and Shandy exchanged glances.

'You'd be in deeper trouble if you tried to pervert the course of justice,' said Samson. 'Shandy is right. You must be strong.'

'I wish you wouldn't tell me that. I'm not strong.' Maureen began crying again. After a few moments she wiped her eyes with the soggy piece of kitchen towelling. 'What are you going to do?' she asked.

'Shandy and I will be going back to London and I shall inform Mr Ruddick's solicitors of the situation. They will apply again for bail, which has been refused so far. I promise I'll do my best for you if you'll do your best for me.'

'Promises. I've had that before. If I'd had ten pounds for every promise I've been given I'd be a rich woman.'

'My promises are good currency.'

'I'll think about it.'

Not long after this exchange Samson and Shandy were driving back to London. It had been a long night and Shandy slept for most of the journey. When Samson stopped outside her house he told her to take the rest of the day off.

'I've got a case I must deal with,' she said.

'I'll cope – with Georgia's help.'

Shandy alighted from the car.

'She's coming along well, isn't she?' Samson asked.

'Georgia? . . . Oh, yes . . . Fine.'

Shandy's delayed agreement betrayed traces of jealousy she felt for the newcomer.

Samson gave a smile which lighted his heavy features with an odd charm. 'Thanks again for all your help,' he said. 'I couldn't have managed without you.' And then he drove away.

He managed two hours' sleep before going for his customary walk round the park. At his office he first checked with Georgia on the happenings of the previous day before putting through a call to Ruddick's solicitors. As legal representatives of the accused man it would be their duty to press for his release from custody by a bail application and, if necessary, to pursue the procedures for a writ of *habeas corpus*.

When this call had been made and he had fully explained the situation he asked Georgia to put him through to the hospital where Hislop was receiving treatment for his injuries. The outcome of this call was totally unexpected. A ward sister told him that the patient had suffered internal injuries as well as cracked ribs and during the night had haemorrhaged. In spite of an emergency operation and numerous blood transfusions he had died. Samson gravely thanked her for this sad news but inwardly he felt great satisfaction. It meant that Maureen would now have nothing to fear from Hislop's threats. She could testify in court on what had occurred on the night when Colin Coomber was murdered and not be afraid of reprisals from a vindictive husband. Nobody need ever know that she had defrauded a bank. The murder would be attributed to Hislop, now a dead man, and the case would be closed. She could start life afresh.

Although by now she would probably have been informed of Hislop's death she would still need support and encouragement to go into the witness box. Samson decided to telephone her and asked Georgia to make the call.

Minutes later she told him over the intercom. 'I've let it ring and ring, but there's no reply.'

'Keep ringing,' said Samson.

Five minutes later she said, 'I've got someone. I'll put you through.'

Samson said, 'Hello.'

A man replied, 'Who are you?'

'I'm a friend of Mrs Hislop.'

'Glad to hear it. Where is she?'

'Where?'

'She's gone and I haven't had my breakfast. This isn't service. If I'm to pay for bed and breakfast I want my breakfast.'

'Isn't Mrs Hislop there?'

'No, she isn't. It's all very suspicious. Another guest heard a noise at four this morning, looked out of the window and saw her carrying a suitcase and getting into a taxi. He knew it was a taxi because it had an illuminated number on its roof. What's going on? That's what I'd like to know.'

'You are not alone,' said Samson.

'What?'

'I'd like to know what's going on too. Goodbye.'

He replaced the handset. It seemed certain that Maureen Hislop, terrified of having to give evidence in court, and fearful of facing prosecution for theft or fraudulent conversion, had made a getaway.

Later that morning he made another call but this time nobody, not even a fractious guest, answered. Maureen had panicked and disappeared and with her had gone the testimony which would have exonerated Ruddick from a charge of murder.

* * *

175

As he was carrying Shandy's workload in addition to his own he didn't have time to spare for lunch outside the office. He sent Georgia to a sandwich bar in Crown Passage. 'Get me anything,' he said, 'except salmon and cucumber. I had enough of that last night.'

It was while he was finishing prawn sandwiches that he decided to put through a call to Mary Coomber.

She answered breathlessly. 'I've only just got in from a WRVS committee meeting,' she explained. 'I heard the phone ringing as I came through the front gate.'

He asked whether she had heard from Ruddick's lawyers.

'Yes. Mr Goldstein told me about what you did in Bath. I'm terribly grateful and was going to ring you as soon as I got back in from the meeting. Is there any further news?'

Samson told her that Hislop had died and that Maureen Hislop had disappeared. This meant that the one person who could prove Ruddick's innocence was missing.

He heard an intake of breath and then she said, 'Is it hopeless? Isn't there anything that can be done?'

'It isn't hopeless, but it's not going to be easy. I shall have to try to find the lady. I'll call you again within the next day or two. In the meantime, keep your spirits up.'

'I thought everything was going to be all right.'

'It still could be all right.'

After a short silence she said, 'Thank you for all you're doing. I know Frank will be as grateful as I when he knows how hard you've worked on his behalf.'

'I'll be in touch, Mrs Coomber.'

Samson knew the odds were against finding Maureen Hislop quickly but he had an idea where she might have gone. He remembered that Pearson, the bank clerk at Bristol, had told him that her father had come from Calais and after marriage had settled in Bristol, but he couldn't recall her maiden name. He fetched the tape which had secretly recorded his conversation with Pearson and played it through. As he had hoped he heard mention of the name he wanted. It was Gengist.

Among Samson's professional contacts was a French private detective called Anton Reynard whose office was in Paris. He and Anton had an arrangement whereby if either wanted information about some organisation, company, society, club membership or private individual in the other's country it would, if possible, be supplied. Samson put through a call to Paris and asked Anton to find out whether anyone named Gengist still lived in Calais.

Within two hours Anton made a return call. An Albert Gengist lived at number 97 rue Leclerc. 'I can't find out much about him,' Anton went on, 'except that he's a widower living alone, aged about seventy, and has no police record. His credit rating is good. He has a telephone but its number isn't listed and I haven't yet been able to get it. However, I do have a contact who can find that out for me if you need it.'

After a moment's thought Samson said, 'No, that won't be necessary. Many thanks, Anton. Let me know when I can return the favour.'

'I surely will. Goodbye, John.'

Samson put down the handset only to pick it up again a few seconds later. He keyed Shandy's home number. A sleepy voice answered.

'I hope I didn't wake you up, Shandy.'

'You did, but it's nice to know you can't manage without me. What's the problem?'

'I'm going to Calais early tomorrow. I may not be back until late. Hold the fort, will you?'

Her voice was less sleepy when she asked, 'Is it the Ruddick case?'

He related the sequence of events.

'Good luck,' she said when he had finished, 'and if you want to bring me back some duty free, I'd like Ysatis by Givenchy.'

18

It was a fine morning with only a few strands of cirrus-like torn white cobwebs stretched across a blue ceiling when Samson boarded a hovercraft at Dover. Within an hour he had disembarked at the hoverport by the Pas de Calais and caught an autobus to the town centre. Here he took a taxi to the area of St Pierre in the southern part of Calais.

Number 97 rue Leclerc was a two-storeyed house facing some allotments. A small front garden was dominated by a huge chestnut tree, the foliage of which must have obscured any view across the road to the allotments. Samson walked up to the front door and rang a bell.

There are some days in everyone's life when luck is in. Today it was Samson's turn to have luck. The door was opened by Maureen Hislop, who almost fainted with shock. When she had steadied herself by clinging on to the door as though it were a raft in a turbulent sea she said, 'Why are you here?'

Samson smiled. 'I've come to bring news. I hope you'll find it good news. You are a free woman.'

'Free?'

'May I come in?'

Like many French homes the house was permeated with the lingering smell of garlic. Its aroma was even present in the front sitting room where Samson was invited to enter, a room which was furnished from some bygone colonial era with ornaments from French Indo-China lining a marble mantelpiece. Samson sat down in a capacious bamboo-cane chair.

Maureen, looking bewildered, perched herself on a stool by an old Blüthner upright piano. 'What do you mean – free?' she asked.

'Your husband was more seriously injured than was at first thought.'

Samson paused to allow her to assimilate the information. Her hand went to her mouth. 'He's dead?'

'Yes.'

'He died – just like that?'

'During an operation.'

'Well . . . I can't say I'm very sorry. He was an evil man.' She shook her head as if to clear a mental fog. 'How did you find me?'

'That doesn't really matter. Finding people is my job. More to the point, will you come back to England? You are free now but someone else's freedom depends on you.'

'Will it mean that I shall have to go into a witness box, go in front of a judge?' she asked apprehensively.

'Possibly, but you won't be under the threat that you might be arrested over the bank affair. That can remain a little secret between the two of us. There'll be no question of you being sent to prison, deprived of your liberty.'

She didn't respond immediately to this inducement. Instead, her eyes roved uncertainly round the room with its mementoes of a past life, its faded fabrics and its furnishings from a bygone age, as though seeking something comfortably familiar on which to fasten for security. In the end she looked to Samson for support.

'What can I say?' she asked. 'How can I explain coming here? The police or a judge might think I did a runner because I was as guilty as Freddie.'

'You are related to Mr Albert Gengist?'

'He's my uncle. I've known him all my life.'

'Where is he now?'

She nodded towards the window, which was covered by

179

the folds of a yellowing net curtain. 'He's out there. Over the road. He's got an allotment.'

'I don't think anyone will question you about doing a runner but, if they do, simply say that you were worried about his health and came over to see him and look after him, if necessary. He is a widower living alone, isn't he?'

Her eyes widened. 'My, you do know a lot!'

'So,' said Samson, 'can I take it that you'll come back? There is at least one man still waiting for his breakfast at Pinetree Guest House. Don't disappoint him.'

For the first time a smile stole across her face. 'I daresay there's more than one. I panicked. As soon as you and your lady friend left I threw a few things into a couple of bags and scarpered. Yes, I'll come back. Can I come with you?'

'I'd be very glad of your company,' replied Samson. The response was entirely sincere. He was glad, not because he craved her company, but if she travelled with him it would ensure she returned to England. Having found her, he didn't want to risk losing her.

'I know it sounds stupid,' she said with a nervous laugh, 'but I need support. Give Freddie his due, he supported me in his fashion. I've always been used to a man supporting me.'

'I'll stay with you while you make a statement to the police, unless you'd prefer to instruct a lawyer.'

'No. I want you. Thanks.' She stood up. 'I'd better go and tell my uncle what's happening. I don't think he'll mind if I go. He's a dear old chap but I don't think he really appreciated me dropping in on him out of the blue. Will you stay here and wait for me?'

'I'll wait for you.'

Previously, Samson had passed through Calais quickly en route for the south. He decided to take advantage of the brief visit to widen his newly acquired appreciation of the arts by viewing Rodin's statue of the burghers of Calais. With Maureen Hislop standing beside him he duly admired the powerfully wrought group of six brave men who, many hundreds of years before, had sacrificed their lives to save the town. Then, after a nod of tourist-viewing acknowledgement in the direction of the ornate Flemish-style town hall standing behind the statue, he hailed a taxi to take them to the hoverport.

After making her statement to the police in London, and voluntarily surrendering her passport, Maureen was allowed to return to Bath. Samson took her to Paddington to catch a high-speed train. They said good bye on the platform and to his embarrassment she flung her arms round his neck and kissed him hard on the lips.

'That's Maureen's way of saying thank-you for all you've done,' she said, releasing him. 'And don't forget, if ever you're in Bath again there'll be no charge for accommodation while I'm at Pinetree.'

'I'll remember that,' replied Samson.

He walked away from the platform with springy step. Although the kiss had been embarrassing it had also provoked a sort of pleased discomfiture.

Back at his office he put through a call to Mary Coomber. When he had finished his account of the visit to Calais she said, 'I shall never be able to thank you enough. And I'm sure Frank will feel the same. Without you he would have had to stand trial for a murder he never committed.' She said some more in the same vein of gratitude before signing off.

A smile of satisfaction spread across Samson's face as he replaced the handset. Apart from sending in his bill, the case was completed. Or rather, his part in it was completed. Various judicial loose ends remained to be tied up like verdicts in coroners' courts on the deaths of Colin Coomber and Freddie Hislop. The inquest on Colin Coomber, which had been adjourned after evidence of identification only, would be reopened and a probable verdict of murder or manslaughter brought in, but there would be no question of the police wishing to pursue a prosecution. How could they prosecute a dead man? The inquest on Freddie Hislop would almost certainly result in a verdict of death by accident or misadventure.

All things considered, Samson reflected, everything had turned out for the best.

For once he was overlooking the fact that Fate, like any powerfully motivated and ruthless body politic, has a dirty-tricks department.

19

During the days following Ruddick's release from custody Samson wondered once or twice why he had not received so much as a note expressing gratitude for having obtained proof of his client's innocence. He decided to submit his account for services rendered. It was posted to Ruddick's home address and read:

To expenses incurred in investigating Mr Colin Coomber's background and discovering the facts about the car crash in which a Mr Vernon Brown died, to ascertaining facts about Mr Coomber's life during the time he lived under the alias of 'Vernon Brown', and to subsequent investigations with a view to exonerating you from criminal charges together with various expenses and disbursements in connection with the above including visits to Bath, Bristol and Calais . . . £3,500

He was mildly surprised when, less than twenty-four hours after the account was posted, Georgia rang on the intercom to say that Ruddick was in the waiting room and would like to see him for five minutes. 'Send him up,' said Samson and there was a degree of satisfaction in his voice. Although he didn't care for Ruddick it was always pleasing to be paid and thanked.

He opened the door of his room and went to stand behind his desk. 'Good afternoon,' he said as Ruddick appeared in the doorway.

Ruddick didn't reply but marched straight across to the desk and tossed the bill for services rendered in front of the detective. 'What's the meaning of this?' he demanded.

A faint flush coloured Samson's normally sallow cheeks. Exerting self-control he said calmly, 'Please be seated, Mr Ruddick.'

'I don't want to sit down. This isn't a consultation. I just want to know why you've got the nerve to send me in an account when you haven't done what you undertook to do.'

Samson said, 'You are disputing my charges?'

'I certainly am. The deal, I would remind you, was that you would obtain evidence that Coomber never suffered amnesia and returned to Mary for the purpose of improving his finances. Where's your evidence that he never suffered amnesia?'

'Do you always refer to your half-brother by his surname?'

'That has nothing to do with it, or with you. Where's your proof?'

Samson picked up the bill and studied it.

'We had a verbal contract,' Ruddick continued. 'Do you deny it?'

'No, I don't deny it.'

'You try to sue me and I'll fight every inch of the way. You have no right to expect me to pay for something I never asked you to do.'

'Without me,' said Samson, 'you wouldn't be standing here. You'd be facing a charge of murder.'

'That has nothing to do with the agreement between us. I didn't hire you to find proof of my innocence. So you can forget your charges. I'm not paying a penny.'

'We shall see,' said Samson. 'Now get out before I throw you out.'

Ruddick turned and hurried to the door.

Samson wasn't a malicious man but neither was he forgiving of those who profited at his expense. He was still

184

considering how best to even the score with Ruddick when a call came through from Mary Coomber.

'Oh, Mr Samson, I'm glad you're there. Has Frank been to see you yet?'

'He has.'

'Oh dear!' It sounded like a genuine exclamation of distress. 'I had wanted to speak to you first but I had to go out and have only just got back. You must think him terribly ungrateful.'

'I do.'

'I'm sorry . . . Mr Samson?'

'Yes.'

'You will be paid for all your work. I shall pay you out of my own money but I'd rather Frank didn't know. Perhaps it's cowardly but I don't want any more scenes.'

'I'll certainly treat this call as confidential,' said Samson, 'but I don't see why you should pay.'

'Please let me. I'd like to give you a cheque personally but I'm afraid if I come up and see you at your office I might run into Frank. That would be just my luck. I don't suppose . . . ' She faltered and stopped.

'What don't you suppose?' Samson enquired.

Her reply came in a rush of words. 'I don't suppose you'd be willing to come here? Today, I mean. There's something I very much need to explain . . . I can't do it on the phone.'

'Won't tomorrow do?' Samson asked. 'I'm trying to catch up with arrears.'

Her voice sounded subdued as she said, 'I might not be here tomorrow. I'm planning on taking a holiday. And that's confidential too.'

Samson glanced at his watch. 'I'll be with you within the hour,' he said.

In London he used various modes of transport including underground trains, taxis, buses, his car, his own two feet and occasionally a chauffeur-driven car. For the visit to Mary

185

Coomber he hired a chauffeur-driven car. He told its driver to wait in the slip road close to the row of town houses at Woodford Green.

Mary Coomber opened the door. 'How kind of you to come,' she said. 'The sitting room is upstairs. I'll lead the way. I've taken a chance and prepared some tea. I hope you take tea.'

Samson followed her up a flight of stairs to a room on the first floor. It was comfortably and conventionally furnished and its only unusual feature was the number of plants round the periphery of the room. There was a cheese plant, a peacock plant, a philodendron, a stag's-horn fern, a grape ivy clambering up one wall, a spider plant and others Samson couldn't name.

'I hope you like Earl Grey,' said Mary Coomber, pouring from a chased silver teapot.

'Thank you, yes.'

She passed a plate of daintily cut sandwiches. 'Salmon and cucumber. I hope you like them.'

'I do, very much,' he replied politely. Mary Coomber wasn't to know that such sandwiches evoked memories of sitting round a kitchen table in the guest house.

She put down the plate and handed him an envelope. 'Let's get this out of the way,' she said. 'You'll find I've honoured the original agreement. It was for three and a half thousand, wasn't it?'

'Yes, but . . . '

She raised her hand as if to silence him and in a voice remarkably firm for one who gave the appearance of passivity said, 'No "buts", Mr Samson. It was well worth it.'

Samson put the envelope inside his coat pocket.

She sat down in an armchair facing him and regarded him steadfastly with dark-blue eyes. He noticed that a discolouration round one eye still lingered faintly.

'I said I wanted to explain something,' she began.

'You did.'

'I don't know whether you've been told the story that woman gave to the police.'

'I was there when she made a statement.'

'According to Mr Goldstein, who's seen her statement, she said that her husband and Colin cooked up an idea to kill Auntie Daisy and that Colin welched on an agreement to pay him money after he had committed that most brutal murder. Is that right? Is that what she said?'

'It's the gist of what she said,' Samson replied.

'I'm sure she was lying. Colin would never plan a thing like that. I lived with him for many years and knew him inside out. I believe it was all that man Hislop's idea. Colin must have told him at some time that I'd be the only beneficiary and he thought that if he got Aunt Daisy out of the way he'd be able to pressurise Colin into getting some of the money she left me. I heard about that dreadful video he made of poor Auntie's death. I expect that, given the time, he would have doctored it to make it seem that Colin had taken it. Thank God that never happened.'

Samson listened in silence and didn't speak when she had finished outlining her theory.

'Don't you agree,' she asked, 'that is what happened? I'm certain Colin would never have been a party to such a vile plot.'

Samson remained silent.

'I knew Colin,' she continued. 'I was his wife!'

Samson broke his silence. 'He faked his own death and took on an alias. He left you.'

She lowered her eyes. 'He didn't leave me,' she said softly.

'What?'

'Well, in one sense he did, but in another he didn't.'

Having listened with quiet scepticism to her hypothetical version of events Samson now began to have reservations about his opinion that through mistaken loyalty she was trying to whitewash Colin Coomber's behaviour.

'I'm afraid I don't follow you,' he said.

She lifted her eyes to meet his. 'The day after the crash

he phoned and told me exactly what had happened.' She paused as if waiting for some comment from him.

'So you knew all along that he was alive.'

'Not all along. There was a whole day when I thought he'd died in an accident. It was dreadful. I can't tell you how relieved I was to hear his voice.'

Samson was now intensely curious. 'What explanation did he give?'

'He was bitterly ashamed at having lost his job and had acted on impulse in swapping identities with the dead man. He said he couldn't bear to come forward and admit what he'd done and that, for a while, he'd live as Vernon Brown and pretend he'd lost his memory.'

'And you accepted such a crazy situation?'

'Not willingly but there was nothing I could do. He wouldn't tell me where he was. I pleaded but he was adamant. I had to be content with his promise that he'd phone me regularly. And he did. And he came to see me twice. But then the phone calls stopped. That must have been about the time he went to Bath.' She paused to take a sip of tea.

'Didn't you try to persuade him to stop the charade when he came to see you?'

'Of course I did. But he was intent on building up another life. He said that when he was ready, and had made enough money, he'd send for me and we'd start afresh.'

'Strange conduct,' remarked Samson, 'but just understandable if imagination is stretched. What I can't understand is why, knowing what you did, you began living with his half-brother after you moved from Temple Fortune to Woodford Green.'

She gave a sad smile. 'I know it must be hard to understand. I felt a bit desperate when he stopped his regular phone calls. But although he wasn't communicating I didn't think he'd completely abandoned interest in me. I guessed that in one way or another he'd be surreptitiously checking

188

on me from time to time. As I say, I knew him well. And I also knew that if I took up with Frank' – she winced as she used the phrase – 'and he learned about it, he'd find some way of turning up again. That makes me sound like some sort of scheming hussy, doesn't it?'

Samson shrugged. 'That's one way of looking at it. Another way, and one I'd prefer, is that you were an astute woman who quite reasonably took advantage of acute psychological insights.'

She smiled. 'That's a very kind way of putting it.' Her smile vanished as she went on, 'But although I could predict Colin's behaviour I could never have predicted that this Hislop man would kill Aunt Daisy.'

'You've had a difficult time, Mrs Coomber, running with the hares and hunting with the hounds, as it were.'

'Very difficult. Luckily I'm quite adaptable . . . Would you like another sandwich?'

'No, thank you. I must watch my weight. But they are delicious . . . When we spoke earlier you said you might be going on holiday tomorrow.'

'Yes, I want to get away for a while. I'm staying with an old school friend who lives near Edinburgh. I want time to think.' She gave a whimsical half-smile. 'It's ironic, isn't it. I'm using exactly the same line that Colin used on me. Time to think. I didn't understand the need for it then; I do now.'

'And have you any idea what conclusions your thoughts might reach?'

She looked pensive. 'The house is mine. I might sell it.'

'And Mr Ruddick?'

'He's got his shop and all those unpleasant weapons. He was alone when I decided to encourage his advances. It won't harm him to be alone again. At least, for a while.'

'I'd agree with that,' said Samson feelingly.

'I'm not a helpless little woman, Mr Samson, although sometimes I might seem it. In fact, I might well go ahead

and back the film package Mr Arzan lined up with Colin.
I shall give it serious consideration.'

A gleam of amusement lighted Samson's eyes. 'Quite
early on I formed the impression that you weren't all you
seemed.'

Her dark-blue eyes shone as though reflecting the expression in his. 'That's what makes you a very good detective.'

Samson finished his cup of tea and put it down on
a glass-topped table beside a small flowering potted begonia.

'Can I pour you another?'

He shook his head. 'No, thank you. As I told you,
I've got arrears to clear at the office. I must be getting
back. But thank you for the hospitality, the explanation
and the cheque.' He stood up. 'And good luck with the
future, whatever it may hold.'

It seemed that the case was finally closed and on his journey
back to the office he wondered whether Mary Coomber was
right and that her husband hadn't connived in a murder, or
whether Maureen Hislop was right, and he had.

But whichever woman was right, Samson was wrong
in thinking the case was closed. The coroner's inquest
on the death of Colin Coomber hit the headlines of the
tabloid press and on the Sunday following the inquest a
large-circulation Sunday newspaper gave a two-page spread
to Maureen Hislop who, it was reported elsewhere, had
been paid fifty thousand pounds for her story, 'My Life
with Knife-Man Killer'.

Samson, who normally took two of the heavier Sunday
newspapers, saw an advertisement for Maureen Hislop's
story on Saturday evening television. The following morning he bought a copy of the paper. It was with increasing
dismay that he read Maureen Hislop's version of events, of
how she had a perverted husband who had, with the man
she loved, plotted to kill a harmless but rich old woman.
She confessed to being in mortal dread of her husband
and said she had run away from the guest house they had

managed together because she was afraid of reprisals from him. However, she had been tracked to Calais by a brilliant London detective, John Samson, who had brought her the news that her husband had died in an accident. There was no mention that Colin Coomber had adopted the name of Vernon Brown or of Hislop's hold over her on account of a bank fraud.

Samson was less than gratified by her unsolicited praise. He hadn't given permission for his name to be used, and the newspaper editor should have made sure that the story had been checked out with him and was accurate. It wasn't accurate because it implied that he was in agreement with her version of events.

He was still brooding on whether to register a protest with the Press Council when he entered the office on Monday to be met by Georgia, glowing with excitement, presenting him with a copy of the newspaper. 'How about that?' she asked. 'Your name's in print and it praises you.'

'I've read it and I'd like to know why they used my name without first checking with me.'

Georgia's excitement evaporated and she looked sheepish. 'As a matter of fact, I told them.'

'Told them what?'

'It was late Friday. You and Shandy had left me to lock up. This call came through. Someone wanting confirmation that it was your case. I said it was. I thought it would be good publicity. The man said you must be a smart PI.'

'Georgia, never, never, never, repeat, never, have anything to say to the press without clearing it with me first.'

'Oh, Christ, I'm sorry. I haven't blown my chances here, have I?'

She looked small, vulnerable and pathetic as she awaited Samson's reply.

'No, you haven't blown your chances. But watch it in future.'

'Oh, I will. I couldn't bear to lose this job. It's the best thing that's ever happened to me.' Tears came to her eyes. 'It means everything.'

Samson reached out and gently patted her on the shoulder. 'Enough of that. You're doing very well. Now get on with your work.'

It was three days after the publication of Maureen Hislop's story that a man turned up at the office requesting an interview. He said he had read the story and needed the services of a good detective. He had travelled from Liverpool just to see Samson and ask for help.

'What is the problem?' Samson asked when, after a long wait, the man was eventually shown up to his room.

'It's our son,' came the reply. 'My missus and I often worry about him and wonder where he is.'

Another missing-person case, thought Samson. He switched on the concealed tape-recorder, adjusted the hour-glass on his desk so that the sands would start running, and picked up his pen. 'Have you tried the Salvation Army? The police?'

'We've tried everything,' the man said. 'He's a good lad really, but sometimes he isn't altogether right in the head. It lands him in trouble.'

'I shall need to know your son's name,' said Samson. 'What is it?'

'Brown. Vernon Brown,' said the man.